Dingo Dog

and the Billabong Storm

Andrew Fusek Peters

illustrated by Anna Wadham

Child's Play®

Dingo Dog was feeling ever so thirsty.
He padded his way down to the billabong for a nice, cool drink.

And who was there do you think, sipping and slurping
all his precious water?

Kookaburra, Goanna Lizard, Kangaroo, Snake and Desert Mouse!

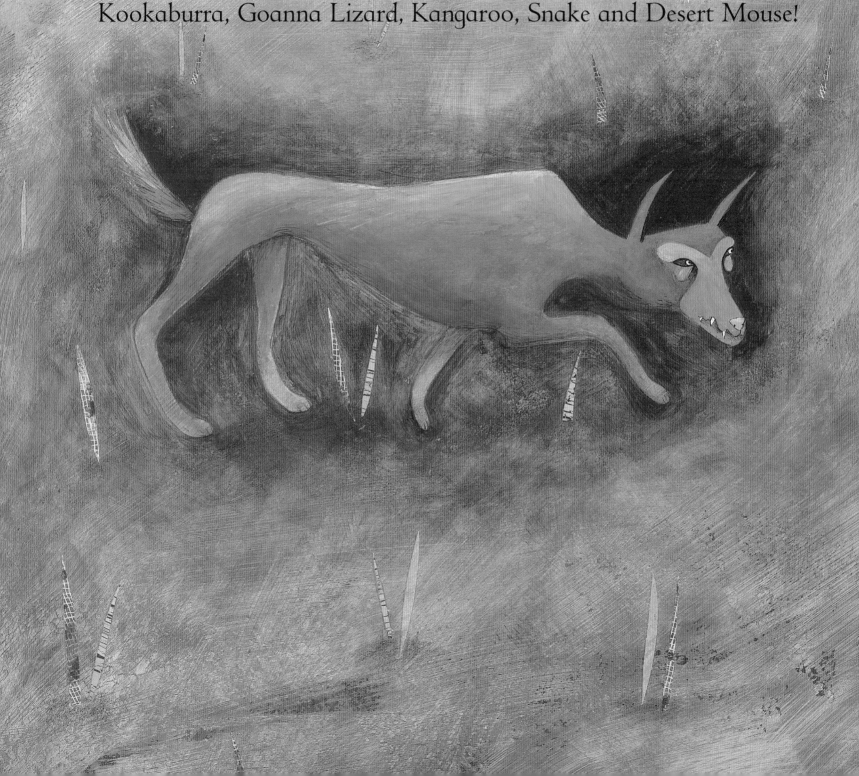

Dingo Dog bared his teeth.

He **howled** until the sand whipped up.
"What are you doing at **MY** billabong?"

He **growled** until the ground shook.
"How dare you drink **MY** water?"

When Kookaburra, Goanna Lizard, Kangaroo, Snake
and Desert Mouse saw Dingo Dog with his **SHARP** claws,
charging towards them, they ran for their lives and hid in the bush.

Later that day, they gathered in the shade of a macadamia tree.

"Dingo's a **BULLY!**"
said Kookaburra.

"I agree!" wailed Kangaroo.

"What shall we do?" said Snake.

"Find another billabong!"
suggested Goanna Lizard.

"No!" squeaked Desert Mouse,
"I have a much better idea…"

The next morning, the sky was blue
and Dingo lazed in the shade of the tree.
He was daydreaming about a nice swim
when suddenly he heard a noise nearby.

"**Hmmm!**" he hissed.
"Whoever's woken me up
is going to be in **BIG TROUBLE!**"

Dingo looked up into the branches of the tree and saw Desert Mouse
and all her family **scurrying** round and **screeching** in a panic.

Dingo Dog was furious.

"What a racket you're making!
Can't an old dog find any peace?
How about I crunch you up
for a little bit of breakfast?"

The mice ignored him.
Each of them had a rope,
and they were tying
themselves to the branches.
"Quick! Quick!
We don't have much time!"

"Time for what?" asked Dingo.
"Have you gone mad?"

Desert Mouse looked down at the dog.
"Dear Dingo, we're not mad, but wise. Don't you know,
the **GREAT BILLABONG STORM** is on the way? We're tying
ourselves to the tree, otherwise the wind will soon blow us all away!"

"Don't be ridiculous!" said Dingo. "The sky is blue and the sun is hot.
There's no storm out there, little mice with even littler brains!"

Two of the mice dropped some macadamia nuts on Dingo's head.

"**OW!** What was that?" Dingo wailed.

"The first hailstones!" squeaked Desert Mouse. "Oh my, it's going
to be a **BIG STORM!** Sorry, Dingo, there's no time to talk."

Dingo frowned. The sky was blue, the sun was hot. It didn't make sense!

Far away in the bush, the kangaroo began slapping
his tail on the ground, until the earth began to SHAKE!

"Here comes the **THUNDER!**" squeaked the mice.

Dingo's eyes **rolled around**, looking for the storm.

Now, Kookaburra began scratching and tapping the tree trunk with her beak.

"Here comes the **LIGHTNING!**" squeaked the mice.

Dingo cowered, expecting the sky to fall on his head.
He was in **DANGER!** What could he do?

He looked up at the mice.

"Give me your ropes!"
he snarled,
"or I will **EAT YOU**,
bite by bite!"

"If you insist!" said the mice.

They dropped the ropes
right by his paws.

Dingo tried to tie himself to the tree.
But his paws were useless.
By now his teeth were chattering
and clattering with fear.

"Get down here little mice,
and TIE ME UP!"

"If you insist!" sang the mice.

They climbed down the trunk and tied
Dingo Dog in knots, squealing all the while:

"The **BILLABONG STORM** is coming!
The **BILLABONG STORM** is coming!"

Kookaburra tapped **HARDER!**

Kangaroo thumped his tail **LOUDER!**

The mice threw **MORE** and **MORE** nuts!

Dingo trembled all over.

"And while you're about it, tie them good and tight!"

"If you insist!" sang the mice.

Snake slithered into the water
and swam around fast, making huge ripples.

Goanna Lizard burrowed beneath the ground,
throwing up fountains of sand, as if the wind had already arrived.

Dingo shook! Dingo shivered!
Dingo shouted! "TIE ME TIGHTER!"

The mice ran around, until Dingo
was done up like a parcel.
At last he felt safe and secure.

"HO! STORM!
Come and do your best!
I'm not frightened of YOOOOU!
You can take the mice and
carry away the other animals,
but you can't touch me!"

All of a sudden, the sounds stopped dead
and a silence fell.

The sky was blue and the sun was hot.

Kookaburra, Desert Mouse, Kangaroo,
Snake and Goanna Lizard all came out of hiding
and surrounded Dingo Dog.

"What's going on?"
Dingo demanded.

"Oh **SILLY, STUPID** Dingo!" laughed Kookaburra.

"Look at the sky! It's blue!" Snake hissed.

"Just like we felt blue when you stole the billabong!" said Goanna Lizard.

"The storm didn't get you, but we did!" said Kangaroo.

"We'll let you go, as long as you promise never to use
this billabong again! You could have shared the water with us,
but greed turned you into a **FOOL!**" added Desert Mouse.

Dingo had no choice. His pride was broken.
He made the promise and slunk away.
Just as he still slinks to this very day.

The sky was blue and the sun was hot.
And Kookaburra, Kangaroo, Snake,
Goanna Lizard and Desert Mouse sat round
their **BILLABONG**, having a nice, long, cool drink.

Example

Interests/Favorites Inventory

Interests/Favorites Inventory for Alex is a fifth-grader who enjoys computers, video games, movies, martial arts, and his dog. He is strong in math. Someday he would like to own a video game store and has done research about having a business. Alex has Asperger syndrome.

Literature

__X__ **Books**

Favorite Books: Harry Potter series, Maniac McGee, any books about computer and video games

__X__ **e-book**

__X__ **Book Club**

Other: Sticky Ninja Academy, Papa's Burgeria

Mathematics

__X__ **Math Games**

Favorite Games:

__X__ **Calculators**

__X__ **Experiential Applications**

Other: Likes working on business math concepts. Alex would love to have his own video and computer game store one day.

Science

__X__ **Animals/Zoology**

Favorite Animals/Areas:

_____

Pets: Alex enjoys his dog Jake and loves to play games with Jake such as fetch with dog toys.

____ **Biology**

____ **Chemistry**

____ **Physics**

Other:

_____

Social Studies/History

| __X__ **World History** | ____ **World Religions** |
| ____ **Politics** | __X__ **Debate** |

Other: Alex has shown interest in units about inventions and innovations. He has shown leadership in debate when it has taken place in the classroom.

Music

__X__ **Instruments**

Favorite Instruments: Guitar: Alex takes interest in the guitar while playing the games Guitar Hero and Rock Band.

Types of Music

__X__ **Rock-Pop**	____ **Country**
__X__ **Soul**	____ **Classical**
__X__ **Rap-Hip Hop**	____ **Blues**
	____ **Gospel**
__X__ **House**	____ **Folk**
____ **Jazz**	

Other:

_____

__X__ **Musical Artists/Bands**

Favorite Musical Artists/Bands: ACDC, Aerosmith, LL Cool J, Beastie Boys

| ____ **Singing** | ____ **Drum Circles** |

Other: Alex takes martial arts classes in the community.

Physical Activity

____ **Fitness**	____ **Wrestling**
____ **Dance**	____ **Tennis**
____ **Baseball**	____ **Volleyball**
____ **Basketball**	____ **Badminton**
____ **Football**	____ **Martial Arts**

Other: Alex takes martial arts classes in the community.

Art

| __X__ **Drawing** | ____ **Ceramics** |
| ____ **Painting** | ____ **Photography** |

Other: Alex sketches for fun and relaxation.

(continues)

Chapter **Three**

Think Big to Get Big

I t is easy to feel hopeless in the face of statistics indicating that students with disabilities have fewer educational successes and greater quality-of-life issues than their classmates without disabilities. Yet every week I meet students, teachers, and families who transcend these statistics and are making exciting educational progress, *from disability to possibility.* This book takes this concept a step further, *from possibility to success!*

I have yet to meet a successful person who did not dream about the future and take active steps to make those dreams reality. Often these people were encouraged to dream their dreams. However, many educators draw a line in the sand regarding the dreams of students with disabilities; they suggest that these individuals are not intelligent or capable enough to achieve their dreams. Sometimes this message is so strongly communicated that the student believes he or she is not worthy to dream in the first place. This is wrong!

Many people have given us great insight into their disabilities or challenges and how they used their strengths to achieve (see Grandin 2011, for example). Many of these important people had rough beginnings. (They're sometimes referred to as *late bloomers.*) The following high-achieving, highly successful people had learning challenges along the way:

- Beethoven's music teacher said, "As a composer, he is hopeless."
- Isaac Newton's work in elementary school was reported as poor.
- Einstein couldn't speak until age four; he couldn't read until age seven.
- Edison's teacher told him he was unable to learn.
- Leo Tolstoy flunked out of college.
- Louisa May Alcott was told by an editor that her writings would never appeal to the public.
- Louis Pasteur was given a rating of "mediocre" in chemistry at Royal College.
- Winston Churchill failed sixth grade.
- Henry Ford was evaluated in school as "showing no promise." (Rickets et al. 2010)

> week I meet
> teachers, and
> ho transcend
> stics and are
> citing educa-
> gress, from
> to possibility.

Interests/Favorites Inventory *(continued)*

Theatre & Acting

____ **Charades**   _X_ **Film/Movies**

Favorite Movies: Loves the Phantom and Dark Knight series

____ **Animation**

____ **Magic & Entertainment Shows**

____ **Stage Plays/Musicals**

Favorite Stage Plays/Musicals:

_____

____ **Acting**   ____ **Sound**

____ **Directing**

____ **Costumes**   ____ **Costumes**

____ **Lights**   ____ **Stage Management**

Other:

_____

Technology & Multimedia

_X_ **Software & Computer Programs**

Favorite Programs: Likes any presentation software

_X_ **Video & Computer Games**

Favorite Games: Currently likes the Halo video game series

_X_ **iPod & iPad**

Other:

_____

Interpersonal Pursuits

_X_ **Going Out with Friends**

Favorite Activities: Gaming

Favorite Places: Gaming Arcades

____ **Telling Stories**   ____ **Telling Jokes**

Other:

_____

Architecture

____ **Building**

Favorite Things to Build:

_____

____ **Buildings**   ____ **Architectural Periods**

____ **Architects**   ____ **Drawing, Drafting & Designing**

Other:

_____

Machinery

____ **Planes**   ____ **Boats**

____ **Trains**   ____ **Bicycles**

_X_ **Autos/Race Cars**   ____ **Motorcycles & Scooters**

Other: Likes Audi brand cars

Fashion/Beauty

____ **Clothing**   ____ **Hair**

____ **Accessories**   ____ **Make-up**

Other:

_____

Hobbies & Collections

Favorite Hobbies:

_____

Favorite Collections:

_____

Other:

_____

Games

____ **Chess**   _X_ **Cards**

____ **Checkers**

Favorite Card Games: Enjoys Magic: The Gathering card game

____ **Board Games**

Favorite Board Games:

_____

Other:

_____

Interests/Favorites Inventory *(continued)*

Culinary Arts

____ **Cooking**

Favorite Dishes:

_____

____ **Cooking Shows**

Favorite Shows:

_____

_X_ **Restaurants**

Favorite Restaurants:
Enjoys most local pizza restaurants

Other:

_____

Helping People

____ **Babysitting**

____ **Charity/Charitable Causes**

Other:

_____

Stock Market

____ **Watching the Stock Market**

____ **Investing**

Other:

_____

Specific Professions

____ **Teacher**

Specific Teaching Area:

_____

____ **Professor**

Specific Teaching Area:

_____

____ **Doctor**

Type of Doctor:

_____

____ **Lawyer**

Type of Lawyer:

_____

____ **Mathematician**

____ **Scientist**

Specific Area:

_____

_X_ **Business Owner**

Type of Business Owner: Video/computer game

____ **Artist**

Type of Artist:

_____

____ **Writer**   ____ **Musician**

____ **Politician**   ____ **Chef**

____ **Business Worker**   ____ **Pilot**

____ **Technology Specialist** ____ **Flight Att**

____ **Software Designer**   ____ **Air Traffi**

_X_ **Video Game Designer** ____ **Driver**

____ **Actor/Actress**   ____ **Mechani**

____ **Other Movie/Theatre Occupations** ____ **Fashion [**

                            ____ **Beautici**

Other:

_____

How I would like to see my interests and favorite
school: Video games allow for free time, break
rewards.

A school club I would like to join is: Debate tean

My dreams in life are: To have the best and mo
local video game store where kids hang out a
gaming nights on weekends

I would like to do this for a job someday: Video,
game store owner and game designer

My recreational interests are: Video/computer g
restaurants, movies

Yet every
students,
families w
these stati
making ex
tional pro
disability

- Tom Cruise, Cher, and Drew Barrymore have dyslexia, which greatly affected their learning and how they felt about themselves as students.

- Walt Disney was fired by a newspaper editor because "he had no good ideas"!

It's wonderful that these people didn't let others stand in their way and persevered. Perhaps they would have "bloomed" earlier if they had been encouraged to dream and take the steps necessary to make their dreams a reality. Better yet, wouldn't it be wonderful if an educator had recognized their talents and supported them with meaningful school experiences? The next person with a disability to achieve greatness may be in your own family or classroom!

Brian: My First Step in Developing the Student Dream Inventory

I first told Brian's story in *From Disability to Possibility: The Power of Inclusive Classrooms*. At the time he was in middle school. Working with Brian then, I used a version of the MAPS process (O'Brien, Pearpoint, and Kahn 2010), examining his strengths, challenges, needs, and dreams as I planned his current and future learning. I particularly zeroed in on school experiences that would help Brian achieve his dream of becoming an entrepreneur. The student dream inventory at the end of this chapter is an extension of the MAPS process. Some of Brian's teachers and I used out-of-the-box thinking and hands-on learning to maximize his strengths and abilities. He benefited greatly from sensory integration experiences, activities that helped him feel more comfortable physically, thereby allowing him to focus and learn.

The next person with a disability to achieve greatness may be in your own family or classroom!

Educational teams that think big about educational outcomes within inclusive environments and plan effectively are able to achieve outstanding results. Although team members may have different ideas about how a student should be supported, everyone needs to be headed in the same direction. The student dream inventory helps get everyone on the same page, zeroing in on what could and should be taking place in school to help the student achieve her or his dreams. Because some students are not sure of their dreams, I've also developed teacher/family/counselor talking points for identifying student dreams (discussed in the next chapter). The focus of both tools is planning for the future: all teachers should design school experiences that not only promote academic learning but also help students achieve their dreams.

As I began writing this book, I checked in with Brian and his mother, Brenda, to see how things were going. Brian was excited and optimistic about his future, acknowledging that there had been stumbling blocks along the way but that overcoming them had been very much worth the time and effort.

In high school Brian became involved in sports. Mr. W., an inspirational teacher and assistant basketball coach, greatly influenced Brian's demeanor, his belief in himself, and his problem-solving abilities. In many ways Mr. W. was not only Brian's basketball

Educational teams that think big about educational outcomes within inclusive environments and plan effectively are able to achieve outstanding results.

coach but also his dream coach. He taught Brian to help others and modeled how to be humble, character traits that helped Brian take new steps toward fulfilling his dreams.

Brian hurt his knee quite badly during his senior year. This was a significant setback, but the things he had learned from Mr. W. helped him carry on. The new Brian believed things would get better and that he himself could make it happen. Even though one of Brian's teachers told him he would never amount to anything, Brian won a scholarship, began attending college, became captain of the cheerleading squad (he is an accomplished gymnast), and organized a dance marathon.

Brian's mother, Brenda, continues to be a great advocate for Brian, as well as teaching and modeling two very important messages: *Everything is possible* and *If you think small you get small*. Brian has been helped by other inspirational forces as well: a dynamic, interesting, thought-provoking, organized law professor and a professor who meets with Brian every week to be sure Brian is learning and understanding the course content. Both professors use visual elements in their instruction, an important way in which Brian learns and understands. Brian has also worked for the Chicago Cubs and is holding a marketing job. His journey toward achieving his dream continues. He values learning, and each day is a step forward.

Dante: Make the Dream Make Sense

Dante is a student with a cognitive challenge who attends a big-city high school. He is social, friendly, and kind to everyone he meets. He has been included in many general education classes over the years, and he and his family have had discussions about his dreams and what he wants to do with his life. Dante's dream is to become a doctor. Some of his teachers told me that this dream was entirely unrealistic and I needed to help Dante and his family get down to earth! However, I promote dreaming, I don't discourage it: *if you don't think big, you don't get big*. What I needed to do was discover the source of his dream.

Dante told me that he did indeed want to become a doctor. I dug a little deeper: "What is it that makes you want to be a doctor?" He replied, "I like what doctors wear, and I also like the tools and machines they use." We chatted some more about school and his life, a conversation in which he eagerly took part.

Then I had Dante and his parents, teachers, and related service providers complete a student dream inventory. Since I'm a big believer in person-centered planning, I readily agreed when Dante's family requested that Dante's uncle, with whom Dante was very close, attend the meeting. Dante, his team of educators, and his uncle discussed the seven guiding questions on the student dream inventory.

The great things that happened during this meeting confirmed my belief in this type of planning and in bringing all the people who have a stake in a student's life into the process. When Dante voiced his dream of becoming a doctor, I again asked him his reasons. He responded as he had earlier: "I like what doctors wear and the tools and machines they use." Dante's uncle, who worked at a local hospital, suggested Dante might be able to get a work-study job in the hospital's central supply division, helping package sterilized medical instruments in heat-sealed envelopes. These workers wear scrubs, hairnets, and medical gloves, just as doctors do. Dante loved the idea of learning to operate the autoclave in which the medical instruments were sterilized and the machine that heat-sealed the envelopes. The school had a work-study program that included supervised apprenticeships during the school day for which students received an evaluation and a grade. Dante's teachers thought the uncle's hospital idea was great. They felt that Dante would be a nice candidate for this program and said they would help make the necessary arrangements if the work-study experience became a reality. Dante's uncle set up the work-study position through the hospital's volunteer program, and Dante's school changed his schedule to accommodate it. Dante was able to continue in the position, with a salary, after high school.

> *I promote dreaming, I don't discourage it:* if you don't think big, you don't get big.

Even though the main experience supporting Dante's dream was undertaken in the community, his dream was born, encouraged, and supported in the classroom. His dream inventory; a committed educational team that included a valued family member; and a work-study experience available as an extension of the classroom and treated as a school course with an evaluation and a grade helped turn his dream into a reality. Dante's dream became a possibility and then a success!

Josh: Respect the Dream

Josh is a positive, engaging young man with significant learning disabilities. As a young boy, Josh's dreams were to be a pilot, an architect, a train engineer, or the color yellow! Josh's parents have always been positive about his potential, supporting him in numerous ways over the years and encouraging him to follow his dreams. Josh's family members are great role models, focusing on his capacities, providing learning support, and believing in him.

Although Josh has strong visual-spatial, bodily-kinesthetic, and logical-mathematical intelligence, school was hard for him and he struggled. One of his early inspirations was an elementary school special educator, Ms. Hinsey, who was helpful, caring, and insightful and created a great support system. Ms. Hinsey knew how to design hands-on experiences for Josh that promoted visual and investigative learning. She also knew that the best way for him to write was by using a keyboard.

Josh chooses to forget middle school, where he had neither a strong support system nor a pivotal teacher who understood how he learned best. His case managers switched every year, so there was no continuity. At one point, he was put into a segregated classroom for students with learning disabilities and behavior challenges and his progress slowed to a crawl.

Redemption came in high school in the form of Ms. Zavell, his case manager, whom he calls a *partner of support.* Josh's dream of being a pilot also came to the fore in high school. Josh's father, Harv, had had a passion for shortwave radio when he was growing up and understood the importance of supporting a child's passions, interests, and fascinations. Josh's family supported him by listening to air traffic control transmissions with him, making weekly trips to the local airport, practicing pilot call signals with him, and taking frequent plane trips to see family members living at a distance.

Josh participated in an "explorer's experience" with United Airlines in which he was flown to a university campus that offered a flying program. He also joined a high school aviation club in which he and his faculty sponsor were the only members. Josh conducted Google searches for information about flying and university aviation programs, and used flight simulators and other online programs related to aviation. He even started flying real planes in high school! Through web searches and a university fair, Josh found an aviation program at Western Michigan University. He went on to excel in college and is now a licensed commercial pilot!

Josh asked me to pass along some advice: in addition to the support his teachers gave him, their *respect* was a pivotal factor in helping him succeed. His parents, Andrea and Harv, feel that general educators need meaningful training in order to be able to educate diverse learners effectively, and that one special education course is not enough. The important message in both instances is to *see beyond the label!* The planning and support Josh's family and educators provided embody the planning triggered by the student dream inventory. Many of us have had naysayers in our lives. Josh had yea-sayers who made him stronger!

The important message in both instances is to see beyond the label!

ABOUT THE STUDENT DREAM INVENTORY

The inventory below is a tool for using a student's dream for what she or he would like to do in life as the basis for creating educational opportunities and action plans that will help turn that dream into reality. (If the student has not identified his or her dream, use the teacher/family/counselor talking points for identifying student dreams in Chapter 4 to help do so.)

Ideally, the educational team members should answer the inventory questions during a real-time meeting. Anyone with an important stake in educating and supporting the student (the student, family members, educators, related service personnel, friends) should be encouraged to participate. The meeting should be recorded, either on audio- or videotape or by a stenographer. Questions and responses could be displayed on chart paper, one question per page. Alternatively, the facilitator (or another person designated to take notes) could create and project a PowerPoint page for each inventory question and enter the responses using a keyboard.

The completed form should become part of the student's file so future educators can also use the information. (Student Priorities/Action Plan at a Glance, a form introduced in Chapter 10, also uses this information.)

Student Dream Inventory

Learner Profile:

1. What is _____'s dream (consider higher education, work, relationships, geographic location, community)?

2. Why does _____ desire this dream?

3. What current skills/abilities could help _____ make the dream a reality?

4. What additional skills/abilities does _____ need to make the dream a reality?

(continues)

Student Dream Inventory *(continued)*

5. What school/classroom experiences would help _____ develop the skills and abilities he/she needs to make the dream a reality?

6. How do we incorporate these classroom experiences into _____ 's school day?

7. Are any changes in _____ 's school schedule needed to accommodate current or new priorities?

Example

Student Dream Inventory

Learner Profile: Angela is a personable and fashionable tenth-grader with significant learning disabilities. Her dream is to become a fashion designer, and her educational team is meeting to explore possibilities and plans that support her being able to do so. Angela is becoming a good self-advocate for not letting her disabilities stand in her way.

1. What is Angela's dream (consider higher education, work, relationships, geographical location, community)?

    Angela would love to be a fashion designer. She would also like to live in an apartment with a roommate in a large city. She would like to be able to take a train to work. For recreation, she enjoys shopping and going to restaurants.

2. Why does Angela desire this dream?

    From a very young age, Angela loved clothes and would draw women wearing various outfits. This passion has continued over the years. She enjoys anything to do with fashion; it is an integral part of who she is. She watches fashion-related television shows whenever she can. She is adamant about making a career out of her top interest.

3. What current skills/abilities could help Angela make the dream a reality?

    Angela has wonderful natural drawing skills. She is constantly designing and drawing dresses in a sketchbook she carries with her.

4. What additional skills/abilities does Angela need to make the dream a reality?

    The biggest need is for Angela to get formal training in design to refine her skills and understand the profession's requirements and responsibilities. Training from and experience with a professional fashion designer would be helpful. Learning how to use the train is also essential, and her family has agreed to teach her.

5. What school/classroom experiences would help Angela develop the skills and abilities she needs to make the dream a reality?

    In sophomore math, students are learning about budgets; as her project Angela could create a budget for a design business. A design class her school offers will help her develop her design skills; her counselor will work this into her schedule the following year. A design apprenticeship in the local community would help her advance her skills and open up possible opportunities in the field.

6. How do we incorporate these classroom experiences into Angela's school day?

    A design class is recommended next year. A partial-day community apprenticeship during her senior year is being explored.

7. Are any changes in Angela's school schedule needed to accommodate current or new priorities?

    Not this year. Next year she will take the school's design course. If a community apprenticeship can be arranged, her classes during her senior year will be scheduled to accommodate the time she spends away from school.

Chapter **Four**

Support the Big Decision

Remember when you were in high school and your parents sat you down for the what-do-you-want-to-do-with-your-life talk? Perhaps they listened to your ideas and options regarding higher education, work, relationships, geographic location, and community. Perhaps, like mine, they told you, "You're going to college," and the discussion centered on that. Considering how many aspects there are to life, focusing only on college is more than a little limiting. (These college-option-only parents may have been told the same thing by *their* parents, so it could be learned behavior!)

Life has many choices and possibilities, and I encourage students to dream about those choices and possibilities. Students like Dante and Josh (see Chapter 3) have no trouble identifying their dreams, and using the student dream inventory as a basis for designing supportive school experiences makes sense. But many students are not sure what their dreams are; in that case you can use the teacher/family/counselor talking points at the end of this chapter to help them identify their dreams.

Life has many choices and possibilities, and I encourage students to dream about those choices and possibilities.

Dan: Shape the Dream

Dan is an intelligent young man who was diagnosed with ADHD at an early age. Dan's passion is video and computer games, and he enjoys social relationships with other students interested in gaming. Elementary, middle, and high school were challenging for Dan, who considers himself a nontraditional learner placed in traditional learning situations. In fact, Dan is very intelligent—he has visual-spatial intelligence and great interpersonal and leadership skills—just not in ways school necessarily values. He was placed in an alternative high school because he hit a student who was bullying him. The alternative school had a behavioral point system similar to a prison—one had to achieve certain numbers of points to receive less restrictive "rewards." The curriculum was also watered down; less was expected of students, and they naturally fell behind. This did Dan a disservice not only in high school but also after he graduated.

Dan's family discovered that he had been misdiagnosed. He did not have ADHD but rather had the attribute of being bipolar; the medication he had been receiving not only wasn't helping him, it was contributing to his adventuresome behavior. When Dan began receiving support that matched his needs, his behavior began to improve and he returned to the general high school. There he proposed starting a gaming club. Administrators approved the club as long as none of the games had violence or adult content. Dan easily found games that qualified, and recruited a faculty sponsor with whom he had a great relationship.

Because Dan had proposed the gaming club and researched the games, he was elected president. He began to walk with his shoulders back and his head held high. He was proud of the club and his leadership position. It was the highlight of his high school career. He made new friends, and some of these friendships were strong and ongoing.

The next step for Dan was accomplishing his dream of going to college. His high school transcripts and educational assessments were not those of the typical student bound for higher learning, but he applied to a university he and his family thought was a good match. A crucial part of the process was the college application essay he was required to write. Dan wrote about his school experiences and his ADHD misdiagnosis. He wrote about being bipolar. He also wrote about starting the gaming club and being its president. He told how the gaming club had positively affected his self-esteem and self-confidence. He even wrote that he wished to start a gaming club at the university! The essay was truly his own, the story of his experiences.

He received a letter from the university asking to see his current transcripts. They wanted to see whether Dan walked the talk and had in fact done better after he began receiving the appropriate support. He had. Dan then received an acceptance letter! This was a wonderful moment and cause for celebration because it signaled how far he had come. Something equally great: the proposal he made in his college application essay was accepted. He would have the opportunity to start a gaming group within the university's computer sciences club.

Dan's dream in high school was to start a gaming club there and to go on to college and start one there as well. Since he didn't know what he wanted to do with his life, I administered a preliminary version of the teacher/family/counselor talking points to identify his dreams and used that information to plan and shape his high school experiences.

Dan's story encompasses all the concepts in this book. It's a great example of promoting a student's passion. He also needed a meaningful support plan for success, incorporating universal design, differentiated instruction, and curricular accommodations. His story demonstrates the importance of ensuring that school experiences are both meaningful and lead toward fulfillment of a student's dreams. Dan now wants to become a teacher and have the same impact on kids that some of his teachers had on him!

My Own Story: Plan for the Dream

Being a student with ADD in the days when "add" was just a math operation was an educational adventure. At the time, teachers did not have professional training in how to support diverse learners. I attended parochial school from first through eighth grade and public school from ninth through twelfth grade. The nun who taught first grade had bird groups in her classroom (a common way of ability grouping during that time in our nation's educational history): the blue jays, the cardinals, and the woodpeckers! Guess which one I was?

I cringe every time I hear someone refer to a classroom group as high, middle, or low. How many people want to be in the low group?

These ability groups were linear ways of sorting students on the basis of traditional assessments, not by viewing intelligence as organic or individual, like your fingerprint. I visit many schools where this practice is still alive (and not well!) today. I cringe every time I hear someone refer to a classroom group as high, middle, or low. How many people want to be in the low group? After I cringe, I am deeply saddened. Characterizing students as smart or not smart is narrow and insensitive. Everyone is competent and has certain gifts. It is not a matter of whether someone is smart or not; it is a matter of *how* he or she is smart (Gardner 2011).

Everyone in my classroom knew which bird groups were better or worse. I certainly did, and being a woodpecker did a number on my self-esteem. For the most part it also made me stronger. However, after talking with many other former sparrows, blackbirds, hummingbirds, crows, buzzards, or vultures, I know this was not always the result. (I may still not be entirely over it. I recently tried to find Sister Viola; I wanted to take her out to dinner and have her call me *Doctor* Woodpecker! I couldn't locate her, but writing this story has been cathartic.) My parents, concerned that I was impulsive and hyperactive in social relationships with my brother, sister, and other kids, took me to specialists. There were two trains of thought. One was, "There is a pill we can give him." The other was, "Get him involved in everything!" They chose to get me involved in everything. When I was in elementary school, I sometimes rode my bicycle ten miles or more to the YMCA, a store, the park, downtown. Those were the days!

In high school, I was a hands-on, investigative learner in classrooms that didn't encourage either attribute. My favorite class was metals, where we got to design and create jewelry, soldering and casting a variety of pieces. The teacher, Mr. Vogel, was an inspiration; I hung out in his office between classes and made a variety of social connections within his inner circle. I did well in the learning situation he created, and it made a huge impact on my education and my life. He supported my learning adeptly. When I tried to cast a ring without success, he watched my second attempt and told me, "Patrick, you're moving the blowtorch around too much and not holding it on the cast long enough. Put the torch on this stand so it will be stable and use a timer." Following his advice, I cast my first successful ring. Thank you, Mr. Vogel, for making things happen and increasing my self-esteem, something I desperately needed at the time!

When I was in high school, I did not know what I wanted to do with my life. Luckily I had a great relationship with my counselor, Ms. Perego. We talked about my interests and passions and she had me fill out some career-compatibility inventories. Our discussions captured the spirit of (and contributed ideas to) the teacher/family/counselor talking points for identifying student dreams I present in this chapter. I am indebted to her for individual, meaningful support. And working with her was fun!

One of the careers that matched my interests was occupational therapy. I investigated the profession and was eager to pursue it. As a freshman in college, while completing a school internship as part of a course, I found an even better match—teaching. I forged ahead on this new career path and my whole life changed.

Teacher/Family/Counselor Talking Points for Identifying Student Dreams

Learner Profile:

The Present

1. What are _____ 's current favorite activities and pastimes at home and how are they incorporated into the day?

2. What are preferred areas of study for _____ in current and former schools?

3. What jobs does _____ like to perform at school, home, or work?

4. What community activities does _____ currently enjoy?

5. What does _____ currently like to do for fun and recreation?

Teacher/Family/Counselor Talking Points for Identifying Student Dreams *(continued)*

The Future

Based on the student's current preferences (above), discuss possible dreams for the future.

6. Dream for where _____ will live and preferred activities at home:

7. Dream for where _____ will go for higher education and preferred areas of study:

8. Dream for where _____ will work and preferred jobs:

9. Dream for where _____ will spend time in the community and preferred activities:

10. Dream for where _____ will spend time for fun and recreation and preferred activities:

Use this form if the student has not identified his or her dream. To refine the student's dream and explore how current school experiences can support that dream, use the student dream inventory. To create an action plan, use Student Priorities/Action Plan at a Glance.

Example

Teacher/Family/Counselor Talking Points for Identifying Student Dreams

Learner Profile: Owen is an energetic ninth-grader who loves physical activity, sports, and outdoor recreation. He has been diagnosed with ADHD. His team is meeting to explore, identify, and discuss Owen's possible dreams for the future so his high school experiences can contribute to his dreams.

The Present

1. What are Owen's current favorite activities and pastimes at home and how are they incorporated into the day?

   Owen is into anything to do with the outdoors. He enjoys swimming, running, hiking, climbing, skateboarding, biking, boating, jet skiing, water skiing, and snow skiing. Owen self-selects these activities and typically participates in physical activity after school and on the weekends.

2. What are preferred areas of study for Owen in current and former schools?

   Predictably, Owen enjoys physical education, science, and shop. He is clearly a hands-on learner. He has been a member of the swimming team and the track team.

3. What jobs does Owen like to perform at school, home, or work?

   Owen willingly mows the lawn and shovels snow at home. At school, he helps set up shop class. He also helps get needed equipment for the swimming team and track team. Generally, he has a good work ethic; however, sometimes he will rush through a job quickly and not think about quality, so he can participate in more desirable activities.

4. What community activities does Owen currently enjoy?

   Owen sometimes swims in a local lake and goes rock climbing with friends. He likes going to a local recreational center to work out. He's also participated in recreational classes and events in a local park. He has run in local 5K and 10K races. He visits a local sporting goods store regularly.

5. What does Owen currently like to do for fun and recreation?

   Fun and recreation and community activities are one and the same for Owen. Here is a list of all the recreational activities he enjoys:

■ Swimming	■ Boating	■ Recreational center activities
■ Running	■ Jet skiing	■ Park classes and events
■ Hiking	■ Water skiing	■ 5K and 10K races
■ Skateboarding	■ Snow skiing	■ Going to the sporting goods store
■ Biking	■ Rock climbing	

(continues)

Teacher/Family/Counselor Talking Points for Identifying Student Dreams *(continued)*

The Future

Based on the student's current preferences (above), discuss possible dreams for the future.

6. Dream for where Owen will live and preferred activities at home:

Owen has mixed emotions about where he wants to live. While he enjoys his current friends and social relationships, he would eventually like to live in a place that has mountains or an ocean or both. He sees himself participating in his preferred recreational activities throughout his life and doesn't think the kinds of activities will change.

7. Dream for where Owen will go for higher education and preferred areas of study:

Owen is unsure about colleges at this point. He is currently exploring areas of higher-education study. Some career options that would support his interests and that he and his family are going to research include:

8. Dream for where Owen will work and preferred jobs:

Owen would like to work in a national forest or park and the career interests he is starting to explore (forest ranger, firefighter, park official, and hiking guide) are compatible with that environment. He also says he'd like his education to take place in a national forest or park.

9. Dream for where Owen will spend time in the community and preferred activities:

Owen's ideal town would have an outdoor recreational store, a skateboarding store, and great restaurants. He'd like the town to have a community recreation center with a pool.

10. Dream for where Owen will spend time for fun and recreation and preferred activities:

Owen says if he worked and lived in or near a national forest, that would also be his playground. He says being near mountains and in an area that has distinct seasonal variations is important to him; he wants to be able to participate in a variety of seasonal recreational activities.

Use this form if the student has not identified his or her dream. To refine the student's dream and explore how current school experiences can support that dream, use the student dream inventory. To create an action plan, use Student Priorities/Action Plan at a Glance.

Chapter **Five**

Empower Students as Members of Their Planning Teams

Teach Self-Advocacy, Self-Determination, and Leadership

To empower students to take charge of their own learning, we need to prepare them to participate in the planning that will affect their life in school, such as their Individual Education Plan (IEP). The tools in this book are planning instruments that welcome students as members of their educational team.

Teaching and promoting student leadership skills in school prepares students for subsequent higher learning and self-advocacy in their adult lives. Self-advocacy ensures that student passions, interests, and input are promoted in school and beyond; it impacts students' lives in many ways, giving them not only voice but choice and self-worth. Self-determination is the desire, the will, and the ability to affect the direction our lives take. These skills need to be modeled and taught so that students can use them throughout their lives. They include leadership in the classroom, leadership in the community, and leadership in making the world a better place.

> *Teaching and promoting student leadership skills in school prepares students for subsequent higher learning and self-advocacy in their adult lives.*

Ari: Promote Self-Advocacy and Self-Determination

Ari is an elementary school student with autism as an attribute. He is constantly on the go, and his homeroom teacher and others have put his energy to good use. One of a variety of classroom jobs given him by his teachers is to return to the library books that have been checked out by his homeroom classmates; there are so many books, he uses a cart. Movement breaks, active learning, investigative learning, and inquiry circles support his style of learning. He has been making positive gains in school academic work and meeting his IEP goals.

However, Ari often enters and moves about the classroom rapidly and noisily, spinning in circles and sometimes running into other students. These whirlwind transitions will not serve him well as a high school student or an adult, and his teachers ask me to suggest better ways for him to enter the classroom and make transitions throughout the day.

When I observed him, I instinctively felt that Ari was unaware how he appeared to other people. I asked whether I could film him entering the classroom, the footage to be viewed only by Ari and me. His educational team agreed, and I used the school's flip camera: *lights, camera, action*. Later, Ari and I met, and I showed him the film. He was dismayed and said so. I asked, "Do you want to do something about it?" Ari replied, "Yes I do." I asked whether I could film him again, this time as he would like to see himself enter the classroom. On the new film, Ari entered the classroom much more calmly.

Ari became a *self-advocate* when he told me he wanted to do something about the way he entered the classroom. He also had the *self-determination* to do better. We continued to use visual modeling support, filming him performing activities throughout the day. From then on, before engaging in an activity (entering the classroom, getting classroom materials, eating lunch, etc.), Ari would use an iPad to view the film of himself doing it properly. A *visual model* of how he wanted to see himself behave reminded him how he *should* behave. How refreshing! How effective!

Marcel: Promote Leadership in the School Community

Marcel was an energetic student in a parochial elementary school. (The principal was a nun.) Marcel enjoyed active learning and being with others (although he liked to be in control). He also loved music, moving adeptly to the beat and rhythm of songs when they were played. However, it was difficult for Marcel to move from one class or activity to the next (he particularly disliked coming back into school after recess), and he often swore loudly to voice his dissatisfaction.

Marcel's educational team and I analyzed what he was communicating through his behavior in a variety of situations. We concluded that he felt out of control during transitions in the classroom and that we needed to find a way to support him so he could and would feel in control. After discussing the Promoting Student Leadership, Self-Advocacy, Decision Making, and Self-Determination in the School questions at the end of this chapter, I suggested we put his leadership skills to use and ask him to manage classroom transitions. We created a new role for Marcel—transition leader!

To make this new role more appealing, we let Marcel use a voice synthesizer, which altered the sound of his voice at the touch of a button. He chose a commanding adult voice. When leading the class in from playground and making sure all the students got back into the school, he turned up the volume on the synthesizer and could be heard by all. Marcel also wore a watch that beeped a couple of minutes before a transition was scheduled to take place.

Tapping into his positive, productive leadership ability also made a world of difference in how Marcel worked with others.

Being responsible for leading students from one activity to another helped Marcel make those transitions more naturally himself, without any drama. Tapping into his positive, productive leadership ability also made a world of difference in how Marcel worked with others. Mission accomplished!

Bridget: Promote Leadership in the World

I met Bridget, a friendly, dynamic, vibrant, fashionable young woman, when she was in middle school. She was extremely social and had wonderful interpersonal skills. She was quick to strike up a conversation and made others feel entirely comfortable interacting with her. She also happened to have Down syndrome as an attribute.

With her mom's and her teachers' support, Bridget had always been a leader and paradigm pioneer, adeptly changing others' beliefs about ability and talent by her example. She forged ahead in an inclusive school, often the first student with Down syndrome to be included in general classes. She created a flyer in which she presented a mission statement and listed the things she wanted to achieve. Having Bridget in their classroom was a new experience for many teachers. If Bridget's teachers did not have the background or skills to include Bridget in the classroom successfully, Bridget and her mom modeled support techniques based on universal design strategies, differentiated instruction, and individual accommodations that supported learning success.

> *People* with *disabilities need to inform people without disabilities about what needs to be done.*

Through the years Bridget's mother, Nancy, and her teachers supported and developed her public speaking ability (enhanced via technology). When Bridget was in high school, she and I jointly presented a keynote speech. It was an honor for us to be able to inform and inspire educators by sharing Bridget's story. She is among the most wonderful speakers with whom I have ever shared a stage.

Bridget went on to attend a university, again succeeding through a combination of her own leadership skills, self-advocacy, and self-determination and university-provided student services. She was enrolled in a child development program where she was given supports and adaptations that helped her succeed. Bridget will continue with further university studies and her goal is to earn a four-year degree.

Bridget continues to speak at conferences and schools. One of her most popular talks is entitled "Dwell in the Possibilities." She and her mother have also started a business called *Butterflies for Change* (visit www.butterfliesforchange.org). They are great presenters who promote self-advocacy by *everyone*!

Bridget feels it is not enough to have people *without* disabilities talk about what needs to be done for people with disabilities. People *with* disabilities need to inform people without disabilities about what needs to be done: "I have a voice and needed to speak up and not let others do it for me." This message is the essence behind everything she does. Bridget and Nancy train people with disabilities to be public speakers and participate in Toastmasters groups. Their work is extremely important and forward-thinking. Bridget has received the National Champion for Change award from the National Down Syndrome Society, in Washington, D.C. She was also recently honored by Clay Aiken at the National Inclusion Project Gala in Washington, D.C.

I wasn't surprised when Bridget was asked to act in the 2012 Hollywood movie *LOL: Laughing Out Loud*, with Demi Moore, Miley Cyrus, Marlo Thomas, and Nora Dunn. She is also being filmed for a segment of an HBO documentary about the Miss You Can Do It Pageant. She has appeared in one other movie, a television episode, and has an agent.

Bridget exemplifies the benefits of developing leadership skills as a means toward educational growth. During Bridget's years in public schools, Bridget's wonderful mom and many wonderful teachers modeled the qualities and importance of leadership. Bridget actively participated in meetings related to her educational program, was viewed as an equal member of her educational team, and was given opportunities to excel and become the leader she is today. Bridget is now positively influencing the larger world through her leadership example, her presentations, and her movie roles as she lives, works, plays, and learns in the various communities of which she is a part. She is a true inspiration for what I do and confirms my strong belief in inclusive schools and communities!

Promoting Student Leadership, Self-Advocacy, Decision Making, and Self-Determination

Learner Profile:

1. Does _____ participate in meetings that impact his/her life in school (e.g., IEP meetings or other planning processes)? If so, describe these meetings.

2. If _____ does not currently participate in any meetings that impact life in school, which meetings could we invite her/him to attend?

3. Does _____ have the desire, will, and ability to participate in meetings? If not, what skills should be taught and modeled to help him/her take this important step in self-determination?

4. What information has _____ contributed in meetings to promote her/his passions and interests? What could we do to help her/him have a voice or contribute? Would creating a mission statement about goals she/he wants to achieve be helpful?

(continues)

(continued)

Promoting Student Leadership, Self-Advocacy, Decision Making, and Self-Determination

5. What classroom opportunities are there to promote _____'s self-advocacy, decision-making, and leadership skills?

6. What community opportunities are there to promote _____'s self-advocacy, decision-making, and leadership skills?

7. Are there any interesting, well-matched school clubs or activities that will promote _____'s leadership skills?

Example

Promoting Student Leadership, Self-Advocacy, Decision Making, and Self-Determination

Learner Profile: Brooklyn is an eighth-grader who works well with people she knows and can be shy around those she does not know. She wants to participate in meetings that impact her (her Individual Education Plan, for example). In a pre-IEP meeting her team has discussed priorities that include leadership, self-advocacy, and self-determination.

1. Does Brooklyn participate in meetings that impact her life in school (e.g., IEP meetings or other planning processes)? If so, describe these meetings.

    Brooklyn has not participated in any meetings in person. Her family has presented Brooklyn's wishes regarding her Individual Education Plan (IEP). Brooklyn is becoming more interested in attending her own IEP meeting as she gets older.

2. If Brooklyn does not currently participate in any meetings that impact life in school, which meetings could we invite her to attend?

    ■ Her IEP meeting.

    ■ Individual conferences with her classroom teacher.

    ■ Meetings with other students (Brooklyn is a cross-age peer tutor).

3. Does Brooklyn have the desire, will, and ability to participate in meetings? If not, what skills should be taught and modeled to help her take this important step in self-determination?

    Brooklyn does have the desire, will, and ability to participate in meetings. The following skills and supports will help her succeed:

    ■ PowerPoint or a similar visual means of communication. She has a strong visual-spatial intelligence.

    ■ Practice sessions with her teacher.

    ■ Collaboration strategies that will help her work with other students.

    ■ Teaching strategies she can use when she tutors other students.

4. What information has Brooklyn contributed in meetings to promote her passions and interests? What could we do to help her have a voice or contribute? Would creating a mission statement about goals she wants to achieve be helpful?

    Brooklyn's passions and interests have been discussed in previous meetings, but she has never shared them in person up to now. It is time for an update, and she could use the student interest inventory created by Patrick Schwarz as she prepares to share her school interests at her IEP meeting.

(continues)

(continued)

Promoting Student Leadership, Self-Advocacy, Decision Making, and Self-Determination

5. What classroom opportunities are there to promote Brooklyn's self-advocacy, decision-making, and leadership skills?

In addition to being a peer tutor, Brooklyn could:

- Be the transition leader during aerobics exercises.
- Be the classroom messenger.
- Be a teacher's assistant (pass out supplies, prepare materials).
- Facilitate literature circles, inquiry circles, and cooperative learning lessons.
- Tell a student "lunch bunch" about upcoming classroom units and lessons.

6. What community opportunities are there to promote Brooklyn's self-advocacy, decision-making, and leadership skills?

Brooklyn could choose which community-center recreational classes and activities she wants to pursue. This would promote decision making and self-advocacy. Brooklyn also has shown interest in a community improvement project in which volunteers plant trees.

7. Are there any interesting, well-matched school clubs or activities that will promote Brooklyn's leadership skills?

Brooklyn has shown an interest in the school pep club and planning community dances. She is considering trying out for the cheerleader squad next year.

Chapter **Six**

Work Successfully with All

APPROACHES TO STUDENT COLLABORATION AND LEADERSHIP

During one of my sabbaticals, a public middle school administrator and I spearheaded a program to promote a deeper understanding of diversity. We conducted a series of physical teambuilding activities that promoted leadership and problem solving. All the groups were heterogeneous, made up of students with and without disabilities. We told the students that each member of the group was responsible for the successful participation of everyone in it. Students who did not have physical challenges (very naturally and without coaching) helped students who did; students with physical challenges helped students who did not. It was elating to witness, an aha moment that prompted me to create the Effective Group-Work Options to Achieve a Collaborative and Cooperative Classroom Community inventory at the end of this chapter. Each option is described below.

> *Promoting learning in a variety of ways strengthens student engagement and understanding.*

Role-Plays

Some students need to represent something physically in order to understand it. Having students act out important concepts from lessons, units, and areas of study strengthens the comprehension of not only those presenting the vignettes but also those viewing them.

Learning Centers

Providing learning center options allows teachers to assess student interests, strengths, intelligences, and favorite ways of learning. Activities can be used to promote various reading, writing, mathematical, visual, interpersonal, intrapersonal, scientific, kinesthetic, and musical concepts. Promoting learning in a variety of ways strengthens student engagement and understanding.

Literature Circles

Literature circles promote reading comprehension and student collaboration. Assigning roles within the group lets teachers personalize and support learning for all students, especially diverse learners. Learning in this structured collaboration is engaging and fun. As students become more familiar with and more skilled at this type of discussion, they can be allowed more freedom and choice.

Inquiry Circles

Inquiry circles (Harvey and Daniels 2009) are literature circles for subjects other than literature. Task forces or research groups with a number of specific roles (researcher, media master, sharer, and publisher, for example) promote learners' comprehension and collaboration, prepare them for higher education and jobs, and empower them to learn for a lifetime.

Cooperative Learning

Cooperative learning is the basis for literature circles and inquiry circles and has many of the same elements. All three are collaborative approaches that value diversity and promote an individual student's strengths and passions: teachers broker information rather than impart it. Groups of three to seven students assume heterogeneous roles such as facilitator, recorder, reporter, and timekeeper. Students share their knowledge with the other members and evaluate their work within the group.

Thematic Units

My friend Annie, a wonderful first-grade teacher in a public school, is the master of thematic, embedded, webbed instruction. For a Halloween unit, for example, she assembles a wide assortment of trade books about pumpkins. Then students:

- Study words related to Halloween.
- Write and share stories about pumpkins.
- Write and share poems about pumpkins.
- Draw pictures of events in the stories.
- Go to a pumpkin patch and bring back pumpkins for the classroom.
- Carve the pumpkins.
- Cook the seeds.
- Put the seeds in jars and estimate the number of seeds in each jar.

Centering lessons on a theme promotes creativity, differentiation, innovation, and comprehension. And thematic instruction is not limited to elementary school. A unit theme in middle school might be the Renaissance; a unit theme in high school might be driving safety.

Multiple Intelligences Learning

Approaching learning through a variety of intelligences (Gardner 2011)—verbal-linguistic, logical-mathematical, visual-spatial, interpersonal, intrapersonal, bodily-kinesthetic, musical-rhythmic, and naturalistic—helps general educators and special educators plan lessons and units more creatively, differentiate instruction to a greater degree, and meet the needs of individual learners more effectively.

Hands-On Learning

Learning needs to be dynamic and fun to be effective. Some students need strong physical experiences—building a model, making a mural, creating a diorama, putting on a play—in order to learn and understand. This kind of learning continues to be important as students become older.

Project-Based Learning

Project-based learning mirrors the way adults work in many professions; it gives students a greater degree of input and the chance to explore a passion. Some teachers allow learners to choose both the topic and means of presentation. Others assign a topic and let students choose how they will present it—write an essay, create a poster, interview an expert. Teachers qualitatively assess student likes and dislikes and their preferred ways of learning and expressing themselves.

Experiential instruction ties learning to closely examined real-life experiences; learning becomes meaningful and engaging.

Experiential Instruction

Experiential instruction ties learning to closely examined real-life experiences; learning becomes meaningful and engaging. Experiential instruction often involves investigations within the community. For example, students working on a unit about protecting the environment could find out what local businesses are doing to recycle.

Student-Created Lessons

Letting groups of students create and present their own lessons fosters meaningful involvement in activities and technology and produces powerful learning.

Teacher-Student Lesson Planning

Teachers plan their instruction with other teachers all the time. They can also get their students' input for upcoming units or lessons (a week or two weeks in advance works best). Students who have contributed to their learning have a greater stake in it.

Games

Learning an academic concept can be turned into a game that makes the task meaningful and engaging. Students can help create these games.

Teambuilding

Teambuilding in the classroom can be both formal and informal. Educators often use formal activities as icebreakers at the beginning of the year. Informal teambuilding experiences are things like a pizza party, a picnic, a student potluck. True teambuilding is ongoing, strengthening relationships over time.

Equitable Peer Tutors/Cross-Age Peer Tutors

Traditionally, a peer tutor teaches another member of the class. The tutor is usually seen as more intelligent in the subject area. But any student can tutor other students, either younger or older. Trevor, a gifted mathematics student, has tutored younger and older students, and this has helped him meet his IEP goal of working successfully with others.

Research shows that the self-esteem of learners with identified disabilities goes up when they are put in the role of peer tutor (Fulk and King 2001). Putting learners accustomed to receiving help in the role of peer tutor can be accomplished in a variety of ways. Students who have special knowledge can be a peer tutor in that area. I know students who have taught other students sign-language, how to program a communication system, and sensory integration exercises.

Active Listening

Active listening is an important aspect of collaboration. It helps students understand one another's perspectives and promotes empathy. It encourages students to support one another even when they don't agree. Active listening can be hard to teach; doing so in connection with students' interests and passions can help. Effective active listening takes practice.

Group Problem Solving

Everyone has problems and everyone needs processes by which to solve them. It's great to start young, in groups. My favorite approach is captured in the acronym SODA:

Situation: Identify the problem that needs to be addressed.

Options: Brainstorm potential solutions for five or ten minutes. Include all ideas that come up; don't dismiss any.

Decision: Pick what you think is the best solution and start there. (Hold the other solutions in reserve just in case.)

Assessment: Create a way to evaluate whether you have solved the problem successfully.

Peer Advocacy

Family members often bring an advocate to an Individual Education Plan (IEP) meeting to present the perspectives and goals they want included. A student should be part of her or his IEP team as well. I wouldn't want somebody to have a meeting about me at

> *I wouldn't want somebody to have a meeting about me at which I was not present.*

which I was not present. However, the number of adults at these meetings can be intimidating. Bringing along a peer (chosen by the student and approved by the family) for support can be tremendously reassuring. Every meeting about a student should begin with a statement by the student (or by a team member relaying what the student wishes to say).

Adult-Student Teams

Students need a voice in their school. Most schools have student councils, but students should also be able to send representatives to school board and administrative committee meetings. For example, one school board requested input from the student body about new playground equipment. Brian, a student who used a wheelchair to get around, requested that the new equipment be accessible to him and other students who use a wheelchair.

Lunch Bunches

With this option, a student who needs support developing social relationships has a weekly or biweekly lunch with a group of students of his or her choosing. A teacher facilitates the conversation. For example, the teacher might talk about a lesson she will be teaching the following week and ask the students to tell her how she can be sure the lesson will be effective for all learners. This lets students contribute to their own learning and prompts them to think about the needs of others.

Gabriel, Christopher, and Jonah: Make Everyone Count!

These days, I meet more and more students with autism as an attribute. Each is an individual, and I encounter a wide range of skills and abilities. Recently, a school district asked me to observe three students with Asperger syndrome in a general education kindergarten classroom and suggest educational approaches. Their previous early childhood classrooms comprised students identified as having learning challenges and disabilities. Now they were surrounded by students in the general education classroom who were good models for listening to one another and working together.

In my initial observations, I noticed that Gabriel, Chris, and Jonah kept to themselves and had not connected with the other students. Their teacher, Ms. Horn, felt they were less mature than their classmates. I told her that a great next step would be to introduce collaborative leadership (pair everyone in the classroom with a peer buddy, for example). I also suggested that asking Gabriel, Chris, and Jonah to lead some of the daily aerobic exercises and Simon Says activities would help them develop collaborative skills, participate more in classroom activities, and initiate social relationships. She welcomed these ideas and chose additional collaborative structures from the Effective Group-Work Options to Achieve a Collaborative and Cooperative Classroom Community inventory. Gabriel, Chris, and Jonah made successful strides in their maturity during the year.

Dixon: Make the Group Work!

Dixon is an "intrapersonal" fifth-grader with technological and mechanical interests. He prefers working on his own and struggles when working with others. One of his IEP goals is to become comfortable working in a group. His general education teacher, Ms. Charles, and his special education teacher, Ms. Argent, have been brainstorming possible ways for Dixon to reach his goal. They have both received inquiry circle training from Smokey Daniels and Stephanie Harvey and think an inquiry circle could be the solution.

Ms. Charles and Ms. Argent form five-member inquiry circles that will create projects for a nonfiction unit about diverse cultures. Roles include two *researchers* who assemble information on a chosen topic, a *media master* who creates a PowerPoint presentation on the topic, a *sharer* in charge of delivering the presentation in two other classrooms, and a *publisher* who writes an article on the topic for the school newspaper. Although Dixon finds working with a group difficult, he has a passion for technology; his teachers hope that performing the role of media master will help him take positive steps toward working well in a group. He can design the PowerPoint presentation however he wishes as long as he incorporates all the information given him by the researchers.

Dixon works very hard on the project, creating his own template for the PowerPoint slides using vibrant images, creative fonts, and animated icons. He also incorporates YouTube clips in the presentation. The other students in the group are very pleased with Dixon's contribution and tell him so. They've gotten to know him and his capabilities in ways they hadn't before, and Dixon has gone from possibility to success in a general education classroom.

Effective Group-Work Options to Achieve a Collaborative and Cooperative Classroom Community

Teacher Name: _____   **Grade Level:** _____

Teacher Profile:

Identify which group-work options you already use, which you could expand, and which you do not use. For options you don't use, consider how you might start.

Role-Plays

____ I already use this option.

____ I could expand my use of this option by:

____ I would like to try this option in the following way:

Literature Circles

____ I already use this option.

____ I could expand my use of this option by:

____ I would like to try this option in the following way:

Learning Centers

____ I already use this option.

____ I could expand my use of this option by:

____ I would like to try this option in the following way:

Inquiry Circles

____ I already use this option.

____ I could expand my use of this option by:

____ I would like to try this option in the following way:

(continues)

**Effective Group-Work Options to Achieve a Collaborative
and Cooperative Classroom Community** (continued)

Cooperative Learning

____ I already use this option.

____ I could expand my use of this option by:

____ I would like to try this option in the following way:

Multiple Intelligences Learning

____ I already use this option.

____ I could expand my use of this option by:

____ I would like to try this option in the following way:

Thematic Units

____ I already use this option.

____ I could expand my use of this option by:

____ I would like to try this option in the following way:

Hands-On Learning

____ I already use this option.

____ I could expand my use of this option by:

____ I would like to try this option in the following way:

(continues)

Effective Group-Work Options to Achieve a Collaborative and Cooperative Classroom Community *(continued)*

Project-Based Learning

____ I already use this option.

____ I could expand my use of this option by:

____ I would like to try this option in the following way:

Student-Created Lessons

____ I already use this option.

____ I could expand my use of this option by:

____ I would like to try this option in the following way:

Experiential Instruction

____ I already use this option.

____ I could expand my use of this option by:

____ I would like to try this option in the following way:

Teacher-Student Lesson Planning

____ I already use this option

____ I could expand my use of this option by:

____ I would like to try this option in the following way:

(continues)

Effective Group-Work Options to Achieve a Collaborative and Cooperative Classroom Community *(continued)*

Games

____ I already use this option.

____ I could expand my use of this option by:

____ I would like to try this option in the following way:

Teambuilding

____ I already use this option.

____ I could expand my use of this option by:

____ I would like to try this option in the following way:

Equitable Peer Tutors/Cross-Age Peer Tutors

____ I already use this option.

____ I could expand my use of this option by:

____ I would like to try this option in the following way:

Active Listening

____ I already use this option.

____ I could expand my use of this option by:

____ I would like to try this option in the following way:

(continues)

Effective Group-Work Options to Achieve a Collaborative and Cooperative Classroom Community *(continued)*

Group Problem Solving

____ I already use this option.

____ I could expand my use of this option by:

____ I would like to try this option in the following way:

Peer Advocacy

____ I already use this option.

____ I could expand my use of this option by:

____ I would like to try this option in the following way:

Adult-Student Teams

____ I already use this option.

____ I could expand my use of this option by:

____ I would like to try this option in the following way:

Lunch Bunches

____ I already use this option.

____ I could expand my use of this option by:

____ I would like to try this option in the following way:

Example

Effective Group-Work Options to Achieve a Collaborative and Cooperative Classroom Community

Teacher Name: _Jeremy Nathan_   **Grade Level:** _Seventh grade_

Teacher Profile: Jeremy aspires to be progressive in his teaching. He successfully uses a variety of group-work options to engage his students. Because of schoolwide inclusive education efforts, his students have become more diverse over the past two years. He wishes to conduct successful group work with all his students and thinks this inventory will help him do so creatively.

Role-Play

_X_ **I already use this option.**

Role-playing is an option for group assignments.

_X_ **I could expand my use of this option by:**

Having a group of students illustrate a classroom concept in a "fish bowl" role-play that the rest of the class observes. For example, a group of students could act out an effective meeting and an ineffective meeting, and the students who are observing could identify the components of an effective and an ineffective meeting.

_____ **I would like to try this option in the following way:**

Learning Centers

_X_ **I already use this option.**

Classroom learning centers include various verbal, physical, musical, mathematical, and scientific games.

_X_ **I could expand my use of this option by:**

Having students create a center around a group project.

_____ **I would like to try this option in the following way:**

Literature Circles

_X_ **I already use this option.**

Literature circles have been very effective in promoting positive group work and literacy comprehension.

_____ **I could expand my use of this option by:**

_____ **I would like to try this option in the following way:**

Inquiry Circles

_____ **I already use this option**

_____ **I could expand my use of this option by:**

_X_ **I would like to try this option in the following way:**

I am familiar with inquiry circles but have not done much reading about them or been trained in how to use them. Stephanie Harvey and Harvey Daniels will conduct a training session in our school, after which I will include inquiry circles in my classroom.

Cooperative Learning

_X_ **I already use this option.**

I have used cooperative learning techniques since I began teaching.

_____ **I could expand my use of this option by:**

_____ **I would like to try this option in the following way:**

(continues)

Effective Group-Work Options to Achieve a Collaborative and Cooperative Classroom Community *(continued)*

Thematic Units

_X_ I already use this option.

There is a schoolwide unit on antibullying (including cyberbullying) and student safety.

____ I could expand my use of this option by:

____ I would like to try this option in the following way:

Multiple Intelligences Learning

_X_ I already use this option.

In planning my lessons, I consider various learning styles and make sure visual-spatial, verbal-linguistic, logical-mathematical, bodily-kinesthetic, and musical-rhythmic intelligence; student collaboration and individual work; and inquiry are addressed at some point during the school day.

____ I could expand my use of this option by:

____ I would like to try this option in the following way:

Hands-On Learning

_X_ I already use this option.

_X_ I could expand my use of this option by:

Having students create artifacts for me to evaluate as part of my assessment.

____ I would like to try this option in the following way:

Project-Based Learning

_X_ I already use this option.

This is an option in many but not all units. Sometimes students can choose the topic and product; sometimes I assign them.

____ I could expand my use of this option by:

____ I would like to try this option in the following way:

Experiential Instruction

_X_ I already use this option.

_X_ I could expand my use of this option by:

Creating new units related to community issues and circumstances.

____ I would like to try this option in the following way:

Student-Created Lessons

_X_ I already use this option.

Every two weeks I help a different student group create a lesson.

_X_ I could expand my use of this option by:

Giving students more responsibility.

____ I would like to try this option in the following way:

Teacher-Student Lesson Planning

_X_ I already use this option.

I review upcoming units and lessons with students and ask for their input. This allows me to personalize learning.

____ I could expand my use of this option by:

____ I would like to try this option in the following way:

Games

_X_ I already use this option.

I use games that I have created.

_X_ I could expand my use of this option by:

Having students create games.

____ I would like to try this option in the following way:

(continues)

Effective Group-Work Options to Achieve a Collaborative and Cooperative Classroom Community *(continued)*

Teambuilding

_X_ I already use this option.

I use "icebreaker" activities at the beginning of the year.

_X_ I could expand my use of this option by:

Viewing it as an ongoing process of developing and strengthening student collaborative relationships.

____ I would like to try this option in the following way:

Equitable Peer Tutors/Cross-Age Peer Tutors

_X_ I already use this option.

I use cross-age and special-expertise peer tutors in my classroom.

____ I could expand my use of this option by:

____ I would like to try this option in the following way:

Active Listening

____ I already use this option

____ I could expand this option by using this method:

_X_ I would like to try this option in the following way:

Teach active listening, model it, and have students apply it in a lesson.

Group Problem Solving

_X_ I already use this option.

It is embedded in a variety of lessons.

____ I could expand my use of this option by:

____ I would like to try this option in the following way:

Peer Advocacy

____ I already use this option

____ I could expand my use of this option by:

_X_ I would like to try this option in the following way:

Learn more about it and explore meaningful opportunities to promote it in the classroom.

Adult-Student Teams

____ I already use this option.

____ I could expand my use of this option by:

_X_ I would like to try this option in the following way:

Explore ways students can provide ideas and suggestions to the school's administrative committee.

Lunch Bunches

_X_ I already use this option.

____ I could expand my use of this option by:

____ I would like to try this option in the following way:

Chapter **Seven**

Keep It Real Through Supportive Instructional Thinking

I have taught at and consulted for many elementary, middle, and high schools. In my ten years as a public school teacher, I taught high school, middle school, and elementary school—in that order. If you are an adult with ADHD and a K–12 teaching certificate, you want to try as many grades as possible!

Community-based instruction was a popular and valuable trend when I was teaching in public schools. Many special educators taught community skills, vocational skills, domestic skills, and social/recreational skills (referred to as *domain areas*) in venues within the community. In my school district, students from the elementary level through high school received community-based instruction.

We conducted follow-up studies with our students after graduation to determine the success of this instruction. We were delighted to discover that over 95 percent of the students were employed post–high school (Brown et al. 1990). This was remarkable because at that time the national statistic was that over 75 percent of people with disabilities were unemployed. Many of our students were also living in the community, either on their own or with a roommate, instead of at home with their parents or in a group home or an institution. This also bettered the national statistic at the time.

Unfortunately, another aspect of the study results was not positive. Our students had empty social lives; when they did venture into the community for recreation, they typically did so alone. Why was this true? Our teachers, me among them, had been so focused on teaching within the community that we ignored the importance of inclusive school and classroom environments for all students. A critical aspect of each student's education is being surrounded by her or his peers, by students both with and without disabilities, from grade to grade. Students typically move from grade to grade, preschool through their senior year in high school, with the same core group of learners, which allows and encourages ongoing social relationships. When students graduate, they disperse. Some go to college locally, some go to college elsewhere; some get jobs in their local communities, some get jobs elsewhere. The opportunities for social relationships are never the same. By not allowing students with disabilities to connect with their chronological

> **A** critical aspect of each student's education is being surrounded by her or his peers, by students both with and without disabilities, from grade to grade.

peers throughout the grades, we make it harder for them to develop important and meaningful social relationships.

We learn from our mistakes. This is why I am such a promoter of inclusive school environments for all students. I believe everyone needs to be educated together, alongside one another, to learn to live together in our world. Allowing all students to learn about and understand the diversity within their own school teaches them to live effectively in a diverse world. When students with disabilities are educated separately, neither they nor their nondisabled counterparts are learning about the diversity in the world. We teach segregation in schools when we designate segregated classrooms, segregated lunch tables, and segregated buses and school entrances for people with disabilities. Students without disabilities graduate with the notion that people with disabilities belong elsewhere in the world because that's what they learned in school. Segregation is still alive and rampant; students with disabilities are being denied their full civil rights. (Chapter 9 discusses ways and processes to combat segregation and make everyone equal members of the school and the community.)

> *Allowing all students to learn about and understand the diversity within their own school teaches them to live effectively in a diverse world.*

However, there is hope. Schools are mini-communities. We can prepare students with disabilities to function successfully in the real world—we can teach community, vocational, domestic, and social/recreational skills—in inclusive schools and classrooms!

The teachers and families of learners of any age can produce future community members who are excited about learning, who have a great work ethic, and who use this excitement and energy to create and experience a meaningful future. Establishing student roles and jobs in the classroom and teaching essential real-world skills such as organizing, problem solving, scheduling, getting around, and handling interpersonal relationships prepares students to live, work, play, and be educated in the community and greatly contributes to their future success.

Jack: Plan Longitudinally in School for Great Results

I'm delighted when I get to work with students from elementary school through high school. Getting to know these learners is a gift, an opportunity to identify and promote skills and practices that make teaching and learning better. My quest is always to find what works for students; that is what I write about. There is enough gloom and doom surrounding diverse learners in the discouraging and disappointing national statistics, the things that do not work. I meet diverse learners every week who transcend the horrible statistics, who make wonderful things happen. It is an honor to study these individuals, their families, and their educators to find out how they are making learning work.

Jack is such a learner. I met Jack in elementary school, and he is now in high school. He has a cognitive challenge, is a hard worker, wants to learn, and is liked by his classmates and teachers. Many of those teachers have served him well. His parents are strong advocates for an inclusive education and vigilant in making sure Jack's IEP identifies true priorities. They want him to be well versed in academic skills and well prepared for the real world. It's what every parent wants for their child.

I have been a consultant for Jack's IEP team over the years and it is encouraging to see his goals and progress evolve. He has grown academically, acquired many life skills, and behaves more maturely. The following priorities have appeared on Jack's IEP over the years:

Elementary School

- Using the literacy skills he is learning in the world (reading community signs, menus, mall directories, and electronic books).

- Following the directions in recipes, the steps of video or computer games, and the directions for putting something together from a kit.

- Using the school library to search the Web for information for a project.

- Working with other students to promote collaboration and positive relationships.

- Initiating and completing a classroom job while demonstrating a good work ethic and meeting quality standards.

- Using money to purchase school lunch tickets.

Middle School

- Applying writing skills to real-life activities. Jack knows how to compose and send text messages and update and communicate in writing via his Facebook page. This is promoting positive relationships and helping him to make friends at school.

- Completing MapQuest searches for directions, understanding them, and using mathematics to determine the relationship between the number of miles in the segments of the trip and the trip's total mileage.

- Searching for songs on iTunes and adding them to his iPod.

- Using money in school vending machines.

- Holding down the school job of getting the computer lab ready for students to use.

High School

- Using a template to write articles for the school newspaper.

- Comparison shopping on websites such as amazon.com for items he wishes to purchase.

- Participating in a community work/study job as a messenger for a law firm.

- Learning to take public transportation to and from work.

- Purchasing and having lunch in the community with a fellow student who also has a work/study job.
- Being a member of the school science club.

These real-life skills are helping prepare Jack for the future.

In addition, Jack is part of a general education classroom in which instruction has been universally designed, differentiated, and individually adapted. Jack and his family have discussed higher education. It remains a possibility. He wants to continue his work-study job and would like it to become permanent. Jack's real-life needs for the future are being successfully supported through an inclusive education.

Harley: Work Together as a Team to Make School Motivating

Harley is a high school student who came from New Mexico to live with his aunt and uncle in Chicago and get an education. His family life in New Mexico was tough: his mother died and his father was battling alcoholism. Harley had begun to experiment with drugs in New Mexico, and his father hoped a more comfortable living situation and a better school environment would give Harley the stability he needed and help him make less harmful life choices. His aunt and uncle in Chicago were able to provide Harley that opportunity.

When Harley started high school, he was energetic and outgoing, but he didn't always apply himself in the classroom. He was also an exceptional runner, and people who saw him run suggested he try out for a spot on the track team. Harley loved the idea and did so successfully. He received a great deal of positive attention from his classmates and teachers for his accomplishment, and his self-esteem skyrocketed. He attended all practices and was very successful in the school meets, helping the track team take first place regionally! He interacted socially with other members of the track team and loved being recognized for his natural ability.

Nevertheless, Harley began experimenting with drugs again with some of his new friends, even doing so on school property. He got caught and was suspended—a big counterweight to the positive gains he had been making.

Harley was a key runner in the state track meet, which was being held soon. The track coach told Harley and his aunt and uncle that Harley could keep his current position on the team as long as he didn't use drugs again. Harley's aunt and uncle came to a meeting with teachers and school administrators during which they talked about what might cause Harley to resort to drugs and how they could stop that from happening.

Together they decided that Harley should be removed from the track team and allowed to return only after he had proved he was able to remain drug free. No one wanted him to miss the upcoming meet, but everyone felt establishing this condition would be effective: Harley was very passionate about track, his talent, and his track team friends and relationships. The plan worked! The next quarter, Harley was able to return to the track team.

Harley's story inspired me to create the Supporting Student Needs Within the Classroom Community questionnaire at the end of this chapter. It contains guiding questions to help an educational team devise a plan to support a student's learning gains.

Mr. McAllister: Build the Classroom Community Through Effective Student Relationships

Mr. McAllister, a well-respected middle school teacher, operated under the belief that *all students in the classroom will learn*. Since everyone is not the same, he knew he needed to differentiate learning so that it worked for everyone.

> *Since everyone is not the same, he knew he needed to differentiate learning so that it worked for everyone.*

In Mr. McAllister's classroom, I saw engaged learners who had voice and choice—options for how they did their work. Students could work alone or with others, use technology or not. As long as students were engaged and interested, Mr. McAllister knew he was helping them make gains. When students were disengaged, Mr. McAllister worked with them to find a solution. This typically was not difficult, since he promoted inquiry and investigation, thereby making learning interesting and fun. Since students helped plan their own learning, they trusted him and enjoyed their time in his classroom.

Mr. McAllister embodies Alfie Kohn's philosophy (2006) that the most important thing a teacher does with a learner is develop a relationship that promotes trust, caring, belonging, and accomplishment. When I showed him the Supporting Student Needs Within the Classroom Community questionnaire, he said he evaluated many of these areas when he tried to make learning work for his students. He also thanked me for calling his attention to student sensory supports. I explained sensory integration and how it could be used effectively in his classroom. I even took him to observe a learner receiving sensory supports, and he became a believer. Thank you, Mr. McAllister, for all you do on behalf of effectively educating all learners in your classroom, those who have special education needs and challenges and those who don't.

Supporting Student Needs Within the Classroom Community

Answer the questions related to areas that could support this particular student in his/her classroom and thus help him/her become a successful member of the community.

Name of Learner: _____

Learner Profile:

Real-World Community Skills

- Are there any real-world literacy opportunities or materials from the community that can be used in the general education classroom?

- Are there any community communication needs that can be taught in the general education classroom or promoted in student group work?

- What classroom and school jobs can help this student develop a work ethic?

- If the student is older, is there an opportunity for a work-study job? If so, what features of the job match her/his interests?

- What school recreational opportunities are transferable to the community?

(continues)

Supporting Student Needs Within the Classroom Community *(continued)*

Real-World Community Skills *(continued)*

■ Are there opportunities in school for the student to practice handling money?

■ Is the student able to tell time independently? If not, could he/she learn by following a personal school schedule?

■ Is the student capable of using today's technology? If not, consider school training and practice in using an iPad and iPod.

■ Are there after-school clubs and activities the student could participate in to develop interests and social relationships?

(continues)

Supporting Student Needs Within the Classroom Community *(continued)*

Student Interests

■   What are the student's interests, passions, and fascinations? Are they incorporated into the student's day?

■   How can the student's interests, passions, and fascinations be used to promote classroom work?

■   How can the student's interests, passions, and fascinations be used to promote positive communication?

■   How can the student's interests, passions, and fascinations be used to promote working with others?

■   How can the student's interests, passions, and fascinations be used to give her/him leadership opportunities?

■   How can the student's interests, passions, and fascinations be used to increase his/her comfort, minimize his/her anxiety, and encourage him/her to take risks?

(continues)

Supporting Student Needs Within the Classroom Community *(continued)*

Environmental Supports

■ Which classroom environments does the student prefer?

_____ Quiet	_____ Working as a whole class
_____ Conversation	_____ An area of the classroom besides desk or table
_____ Working alone	_____ A setting other than the classroom such as the library
_____ Working in a small group	_____ Being able to work to music
_____ Working in a large group	

■ What position does the student prefer in the classroom?

_____ Front, near the teacher

_____ Center

_____ Rear

_____ Near peers who are good models. If so, identify the peers: _____.

Communication Supports

■ Does the student have the communication skills necessary to accomplish the following actions? If not, how would you recommend she/he develop those skills?

- Gain positive attention

  Recommendations:

- Participate in a favorite activity or obtain a desired object

  Recommendations:

- Move from one activity to another

  Recommendations:

- Protest constructively

  Recommendations:

■ Do others acknowledge and respect these communications?

(continues)

Supporting Student Needs Within the Classroom Community *(continued)*

Choice/Control Supports

■ What does the student value? Are these things available to him/her?

■ How often does the student get to participate in a preferred activity without having to earn it?

■ Does the student have some control and choice over her/his schedule and activities?

■ Does the student have the same access to basic needs (food, drink, privacy) that other students do?

■ Who does the student like? Does the student get to spend time with this person/these people?

■ Does the student have any meaningful relationships? If not, how could he/she be encouraged to build them?

(continues)

Supporting Student Needs Within the Classroom Community *(continued)*

Teaching Supports

■ Are staff members trained to provide support? Do they have the necessary resources?

■ Under what conditions does the student need teacher support?

    ____ More difficult tasks

    ____ Less difficult tasks

    ____ Boring or repetitive tasks

    ____ Lengthy tasks

■ Are there classroom fixtures or activities that can support the student (e.g., a student who needs to move about frequently could be asked to deliver/pick up things from the school office)?

Sensory Supports

■ Is the student in any one position for too long? If so, what are some viable alternatives?

■ Does the student have active learning options when she/he needs them?

■ Are alternate environments such as using the library to complete work available to all students?

■ Are there seating options such as cushions, therapy balls, and T-stools?

(continues)

Supporting Student Needs Within the Classroom Community (continued)

Sensory Supports (continued)

■ Are there sensory supports such as stress balls that the student can manipulate?

■ Are there sensory supports such as hard candy that a student can taste?

■ Are there writing instrument options, including different sizes and grips?

Physiological Supports

■ Is the student currently using any medications? Are they effective? Should their use or dosage be reevaluated? Are there any other issues that affect the student's learning?

■ Are there medical conditions that impact the student's ability to learn?

■ Is the student using recreational drugs? If so, what are the effects on school and learning?

(continues)

Supporting Student Needs Within the Classroom Community *(continued)*

Physiological Supports *(continued)*

- Does the student have any allergies?

- Is the student in any physical distress?

- Is the student getting enough sleep? Nutrition?

Based on the answers to the questions and the information collected, what are the best ways to support _____?

Example

Supporting Student Needs Within the Classroom Community

Answer the questions related to areas that could support this particular student in his/her classroom and thus help him/her become a successful member of the community.

Name of Learner: _____Adamo_____

Learner Profile: Adamo is a third-grader with autism who is working on literacy, communication, and collaboration skills in an inclusive classroom. His educational team is discussing supports that will help him be successful both in school and in the community.

Real-World Community Skills

- Are there any real-world literacy opportunities or materials from the community that can be used in the general education classroom?

  Adamo has emerging literacy skills. In addition to the literacy supports he is receiving in his inclusive classroom curriculum, we are taking advantage of literacy opportunities in the school building: signs in the hallways, library, and cafeteria, as well as printed lunch menus.

- Are there any community communication needs that can be taught in the general education classroom or promoted in student group work?

  Adamo is learning how to construct a message, send it, and respond to questions or comments on his iPad.

- What classroom and school jobs can help this student develop a work ethic?

  Adamo is a rotating classroom messenger/table cleaner/computer preparer. He is also responsible for cleaning his desk. He is learning to complete these tasks quickly and effectively.

- If the student is older, is there an opportunity for a work-study job? If so, what features of the job match his interests?

  This will be explored in the future.

- What school recreational opportunities are transferable to the community?

  Adamo is learning playground games during recess. He has pictograms (which his parents helped create) that show the steps of the games, which he can use when he teaches the games to his friends in the community.

(continues)

Supporting Student Needs Within the Classroom Community *(continued)*

Real-World Community Skills *(continued)*

- Are there opportunities in school for the student to practice handling money?

    Lunch in the cafeteria is obtained with a ticket. In the afternoon, Adamo chooses and purchases a drink from a vending machine.

- Is the student able to tell time independently? If not, could he learn by following a personal school schedule?

    Preparing a personal schedule for Adamo to follow is a great idea and will be implemented.

- Is the student capable of using today's technology? If not, consider school training and practice in using an iPad and iPod.

    Adamo uses an iPad to help him communicate. He loves the computer and age-appropriate software.

- Are there after-school clubs and activities the student could participate in to develop interests and social relationships?

    Adamo could try out for before-school intramural sports teams. The middle school he will soon be attending has a physical education club offering rotating activities such as volleyball, badminton, and soccer. The club is open to all.

(continues)

Supporting Student Needs Within the Classroom Community *(continued)*

Student Interests

- What are the student's interests, passions, and fascinations? Are they incorporated into the student's day?

  Adamo mainly likes technology and sports. He uses his iPad and other types of technology throughout the day. He could be encouraged to try out for an intramural sports team.

- How can the student's interests, passions, and fascinations be used to promote classroom work?

  Adamo loves to use the iPad and the computer; when he uses them to complete schoolwork, he does quite well. Adamo also loves exploring sports software during his free time.

- How can the student's interests, passions, and fascinations be used to promote positive communication?

  Adamo's eagerness to use his iPad is an incentive for him to communicate.

- How can the student's interests, passions, and fascinations be used to promote working with others?

  The other students in the class love Adamo's iPad and understand that it helps him communicate when he is a member of a group. Many of his classmates share his love for sports.

- How can the student's interests, passions, and fascinations be used to give him leadership opportunities?

  Adamo has used his iPad to remind students about the classroom schedule and deliver weather reports. He also helped create a classroom sports bulletin board.

- How can the student's interests, passions, and fascinations be used to increase his comfort, minimize his anxiety, and encourage him to take risks?

  Adamo is naturally comfortable and not anxious; he doesn't hesitate to meet expectations and initiate communication.

(continues)

Supporting Student Needs Within the Classroom Community *(continued)*

Environmental Supports

■ Which classroom environments does the student prefer?

_X_ Quiet

____ Conversation

_X_ Working alone

____ Working in a small group

____ Working in a large group

____ Working as a whole class

____ An area of the classroom besides desk or table

____ A setting other than the classroom such as the library

____ Being able to work to music

Adamo typically chooses to work alone but is acclimating to working with others. It is important he learns to work successfully with a variety of students in the classroom, as these experiences will prepare him for the future.

■ What position does the student prefer in the classroom?

_X_ Front, near the teacher

_X_ Center

_X_ Rear

_X_ Near peers who are good models. If so, identify the peers: _____

Adamo can work anywhere in the classroom.

Communication Supports

■ Does the student have the communication skills necessary to accomplish the following actions? If not, how would you recommend he develop those skills?

Adamo is able to accomplish all the actions below with his current communication skills, although we haven't seen him protest anything.

● Gain positive attention
Recommendations:

● Participate in a favorite activity or obtain a desired object
Recommendations:

● Move from one activity to another
Recommendations:

● Protest constructively
Recommendations:

■ Do others acknowledge and respect these communications? **Yes**

(continues)

Supporting Student Needs Within the Classroom Community *(continued)*

Choice/Control Supports

■   What does the student value? Are these things available to him?

Technology and sports are areas he values the most, and they are readily available.

■   How often does the student get to participate in a preferred activity without having to earn it?

Preferred activities are always in Adamo's daily schedule.

■   Does the student have some control and choice over his schedule and activities?

When Adamo finishes his classroom responsibilities, he has free time to do what he wants.

■   Does the student have the same access to basic needs (food, drink, privacy) that other students do?

Yes

■   Who does the student like? Does the student get to spend time with this person/these people?

Fernando is Adamo's closest friend. They spend time together every day on the playground and at lunch.

■   Does the student have any meaningful relationships? If not, how could he be encouraged to build them?

Adamo has a meaningful relationship with Fernando. He's working on developing additional relationships during recess and classroom group work.

(continues)

Supporting Student Needs Within the Classroom Community *(continued)*

Teaching Supports

■ Are staff members trained to provide support? Do they have the necessary resources?

Yes, the general educator, special educator, speech therapist, and para-educator know how to support Adamo's iPad use, so there is consistency.

■ Under what conditions does the student need teacher support?

As long as his iPad and computer are working correctly and Adamo knows what is expected of him, he needs about the same degree of support as any other student.

_____ More difficult tasks

_____ Less difficult tasks

_____ Boring or repetitive tasks

_____ Lengthy tasks

■ Are there classroom fixtures or activities that support the student (e.g., a student who needs to move about frequently could be asked to deliver/pick up things from the school office)?

Adamo does fine with the supports that are automatically part of his schedule, and he is able to choose them during his free time. He generally likes most classroom activities.

Sensory Supports

■ Is the student in any one position for too long? If so, what are some viable alternatives?

The classroom schedule is active enough that Adamo changes positions regularly; he can move about on his own if he needs to.

■ Does the student have active learning options when he needs them?

Yes; Adamo's classroom messenger job is active, and he also helps his teacher in other ways from time to time.

■ Are alternate environments such as using the library to complete work available to all students?

Yes; the teacher regularly offers all students the option to work in the library.

■ Are there seating options such as cushions, therapy balls, and T-stools?

Yes; the classroom contains a number of cushions and two therapy balls. Adamo knows the guidelines for using them and does so when he needs to.

■ Are there sensory supports such as stress balls that the student can manipulate?

The teacher has a basket of manipulatives, including stress balls and widgets, that any student can use (within classroom guidelines).

(continues)

Supporting Student Needs Within the Classroom Community *(continued)*

Sensory Supports *(continued)*

■ Are there sensory supports such as hard candy that a student can taste?

Yes; there is peppermint and cinnamon candy available.

■ Are there writing instrument options, including different sizes and grips? Yes.

Physiological Supports

■ Is the student currently using any medications? Are they effective? Should their use or dosage be reevaluated? Are there any other issues that affect the student's learning?

Adamo is currently not taking any medications.

■ Are there medical conditions that impact the student's ability to learn? No.

■ Is the student using recreational drugs? If so, what are the effects on school and learning? No.

■ Does the person have any allergies? No

■ Is the student in any physical distress? No.

■ Is the student getting enough sleep? Yes. Nutrition? Yes.

■ Based on the answers to the questions and the information collected, what are the best ways to support Adamo?

Explore software for Adamo's iPad that enhances literacy. Expand his vocabulary and encourage reading about high-interest topics such as sports.

Introduce new playground games during recess.

Identify additional places where Adamo can use money, such as buying school supplies in the school office.

Implement a personal schedule for Adamo and teach him how to use it throughout the day.

Have Adamo show other students how to use the iPad.

Register Adamo for intramurals.

Research the middle school physical education club.

Use the Effective Group-Work Options to Achieve a Collaborative and Cooperative Classroom Community survey to develop new student collaboration options in the classroom.

Meet with Adamo to explore a greater range of choices during his free time.

Identify other classroom jobs that involve active learning.

Chapter **Eight**

Promote and Develop Membership in the School and Wider Communities

Educators are preparing students for their future. Education should lead to positive life opportunities for all learners. This concept is so important that it is part of the law pertaining to students who receive special education services: students with disabilities are required to have an Individual Transition Plan at age fourteen (IDEA 2004).

However, some schools separate life skills planning and preparation for students with IEPs from work-study programs geared toward the general education population. This is unfortunate because most work-study programs include longstanding partnerships with businesses and other potential employers in the community. These resources should be pooled on behalf of all students. It's also unfortunate that many educators assume students with disabilities will never go to college or other forms of higher education. These practices clearly limit the opportunities of students who have IEPs and promote further segregated teaching and learning practices.

Integrated schools and communities value diversity and offer membership to all.

Chapters 3 and 4 of this book show how important it is for schools to support students' dreams and help students who have not yet identified their dreams and aspirations to do so. This chapter addresses students' connection with their school community and the community in which they live. Do the school's classrooms, library, cafeteria, and playgrounds and the community's restaurants, supermarkets, shops, movie theaters, and parks know every student and welcome her or him as part of the community, a member rather than a visitor? Integrated schools and communities value diversity and offer membership to all—they are, as the theme song for the television show *Cheers* has it, places "where everybody knows your name."

In my neighborhood is a coffee shop called The Daily Grind, owned and managed by a young couple named Raphael and Becky. When I'm home, it's my first stop every morning. I'm greeted by name and don't even need to order; I'm a creature of habit, and they know what I want. However, I travel a lot giving presentations and doing consultations, so sometimes I don't visit The Daily Grind for days or even weeks at a time. When I come in after having been away, Raphael and Becky greet me extra warmly: "Patrick, we've missed you! Where have you been?" I'm treated like family and love going there.

Everything seems better when I do. Everyone needs places and situations in their life that support them this way.

Angelica: Keep and Promote Relationships

Angelica is a high school senior who enjoys music, science, video games, movies, and her boyfriend. She likes being part of the community. She also has significant learning disabilities as an attribute. Through a work-study program she works in the library of the local university three days a week.

Initially, her educational team (Angelica, her family, her teachers, her speech therapist, and her counselor) considered whether Angelica might work in the library full time, in which case she would no longer be spending any time in high school. They discussed the consequences:

- She wouldn't be able to take an earth science course, a metals art course, or a physical education elective in which students create and follow a personal exercise program.
- She'd have to give up being a member of the science club.
- She wouldn't be able to have lunch in the cafeteria with her friends and her boyfriend.
- She could no longer use the school library.
- She wouldn't be able to continue the relationships she had with the other students in her classes.

These classes and activities gave Angelica a sense of belonging, being a member of the school community. If social relationships she'd been part of in high school were to have a chance of continuing, they shouldn't be taken away before she graduated. The work-study opportunity was important, but the team needed to find a balance. Angelica remained a member of both her school community and her work community.

To ease Angelica's integration into the wider community, her work-study teacher set up the following program:

- Angelica has lunch with co-workers from the library on the three days a week she works there.
- Once a week Angelica works out at a local health club with her boyfriend and another friend after work.
- After her workout she goes to the grocery store next to the health club and buys items she needs at home.

Angelica's team focused on her needs both in school and in the community. They helped her retain school relationships and opportunities and promoted opportunities that would help her become a full member of the community.

Bill: Make Life Opportunities Work

Bill was my student when I was a high school teacher. He liked organized sports and enjoyed going to restaurants. He was a member of the high school football team and worked hard at practices and games. He also has a mild cognitive challenge. He was respected by his classmates and treated everyone in a natural, friendly manner.

When Bill and his family had the what-do-you-want-to-do-with-your-life talk, he said he'd like to have a job. His family and I discussed a part-time work-study job as part of Bill's educational program. Bill's stipulation regarding the kind of work he wanted to do was, "I want to work with guys." (This wasn't surprising considering his interests. And he often came to school wearing a hard hat!)

One of the job-training sites in the work-study program was the local veterans' hospital. We'd placed students in various departments—admissions, the pharmacy, central supply—but never the loading dock. When Bill told me he wanted to work with guys, I paid the loading dock a visit. When I got there and noticed that the men were wearing hard hats, I thought, *This could be it!* And it turned out the loading dock was ready and willing for Bill.

I'll never forget Bill's first day. The men on the loading dock were tickled that Bill was wearing his own hard hat; there was instant rapport. All I had to do was step out of the way and let it happen! Bill had a great work ethic and did his job extremely well. The men quickly began fighting over who got to work with Bill. They all wanted him on their loading and pickup teams. (It's nice to be popular at work!)

It wasn't long before Bill's co-workers wanted him to go out with them to a nearby bar after work. Bill was of legal age, and this was a wonderful opportunity for him to socialize. I may be the only teacher in the world to have been given permission to teach safe-drinking skills on location! This may seem a bit controversial, but why shouldn't Bill have the same social opportunities as other young people his age? Isn't it better that he has social relationships with the people he works with? Isn't it better that he knows how to drink responsibly? Bill has the same rights and responsibilities as anyone else; anything else is civil rights discrimination.

Being both a member of the high school football team and an employee of the veterans' hospital were wonderful opportunities for Bill to learn from others. The relationships he made were integral to his education. Oh, yes. The veterans' hospital hired Bill permanently. He's still working there and has received a gold watch for his many years of successful service!

Bill has the same rights and responsibilities as anyone else; anything else is civil rights discrimination.

Developing Student Presence in the School and Wider Communities

To be successful in the world, all students, including those with disabilities, need to be members of their school and wider communities. This is difficult to accomplish when they only function in segregated environments in the school and community. This questionnaire highlights inclusive membership opportunities in school that promote future success in the world.

Learner Profile:

1. During the student's school day, in what general education environments and areas is he/she a member and actively part of activities with other students?

2. What general education school memberships need to be strengthened?

3. When the student is not in school, in what general community/neighborhood environments is the student a member and actively part of activities with other people?

(continues)

Developing Student Presence in the School and Wider Communities *(continued)*

4. What general community/neighborhood memberships need to be strengthened?

5. Does the student come to school by segregated transportation? If so, what needs to be done so that he/she can come to school on a general school bus?

6. Does the student enter the school through a separate entrance for students with disabilities? If so, what needs to be done so that she/he is able to use the general entrance?

7. What instruction is the student receiving in segregated classes/classrooms? How can his/her instruction become more inclusive?

(continues)

Developing Student Presence in the School and Wider Communities *(continued)*

8. What related services is the student receiving in a segregated environment? How can these services be integrated into the general classroom?

9. Does the student sit at a separate lunch table reserved for students with disabilities? If so, what can be done to change that?

10. Does the student participate in after-school clubs or activities? If not, what clubs or activities might she/he be interested in pursuing?

Example

Developing Student Presence in the School and Wider Communities

To be successful in the world, all students, including those with disabilities, need to be members of their school and wider communities. This is difficult to accomplish when they only function in segregated environments in the school and community. This questionnaire highlights inclusive membership opportunities in school that promote future success in the world.

Learner Profile: Henry is a fourth-grader who likes sports and music. He has a cognitive challenge. His educational team is meeting to create a more inclusive plan for his education.

1. During the student's school day, in what general education environments and areas is he a member and actively part of activities with other students?

    Henry is in general education settings for physical education, art, and music. He also mingles with the general student body during recess and lunch. This is a mainstreaming model.

2. What general education school memberships need to be strengthened?

    Henry is doing well in the above general environments, and his team wants him to spend more time in general education settings. He will switch to a general education homeroom and receive adaptive support in general education science, social studies, and speech classes for the rest of the year. Next year Henry will be in general education classrooms for all subjects. His teachers will be trained in inclusive education practice during the summer and be given additional planning time next year to apply what they've learned.

3. When the student is not in school, in what general community/neighborhood environments is he a member and actively part of activities with other people?

    Henry enjoys playing soccer with other children in his neighborhood and is on a parks-and-recreation district team. He practices frequently. Henry is also learning to play the guitar and takes lessons at the local community center. He is preparing for a recital in which he will play guitar, both individually and with other students.

4. What general community/neighborhood memberships need to be strengthened?

    Henry wants to play guitar in a band being formed by some of the students at the community center. His parents have offered to provide practice space for the band in their basement.

5. Does the student come to school by segregated transportation? If so, what needs to be done so that he can come to school on a general school bus?

    Henry does get to school in a separate van. He has been teased in the past on the general school bus and once hit another student. His team is exploring whether Henry can be given priority seating next to good student role models and near the adult bus monitor.

(continues)

Developing Student Presence in the School and Wider Communities *(continued)*

6. Does the student enter the school through a separate entrance for students with disabilities? If so, what needs to be done so that he is able to use the general entrance?

For years, Henry has entered school through a side entrance near a 'special education wing' of the school. When he begins riding the general bus again, he will use the main entrance along with all the other students on the bus.

7. What instruction is the student receiving in segregated classes/classrooms? How can his instruction become more inclusive?

Currently Henry is in segregated environments for language arts, reading, math, social studies, and science. For the remainder of the year he will be placed in general education environments for social studies and science. Next year Henry will receive all his instruction in general education classrooms.

8. What related services is the student receiving in a segregated environment? How can these services be integrated into the general classroom?

Throughout his years in school, Henry has been pulled from the classroom for speech therapy. For the remainder of this year and all next year, his speech therapist will work with him in the general education settings while the other students are working on other projects.

9. Does the student sit at a separate lunch table reserved for students with disabilities? If so, what can be done to change that?

During lunch, Henry sits with two of his friends from the community soccer league; these boys do not receive special education services.

10. Does the student participate in after-school clubs or activities? If not, what clubs or activities might he be interested in pursuing?

Henry loves soccer and is interested in being on the school soccer team. He attends all the school's soccer games and will try out for the soccer team next year.

Chapter **Nine**

Destroy Prejudice and Promote Diversity Education and Experience

Schools often hire me to provide disability awareness education and conduct related activities. Many administrators have a preconceived notion of disability awareness education—perhaps a "disability day" during which students without disabilities experience what it would be like to have a sensory or physical disability (simulating blindness by putting on a blindfold, deafness by inserting a pair of earplugs, cerebral palsy by wearing weights on their arms and legs and using a wheelchair). I find these types of lessons and activities largely ceremonial and counterproductive; they make differences stand out rather than help students understand and celebrate the ways in which individuals are diverse.

> *Everyone needs to learn that someone who may look, get around, or communicate differently—or look the same but learn differently—is more similar to than different from every other human being.*

A better way to heighten disability awareness is to have students look within. Every student has talents and every student has challenges. I have never met a student with gifts who did not have challenges. I have never met a student with a disability who did not have gifts. Allowing students to discover and share both their talents and their challenges during a reflective lesson promotes not only sensitivity to diversity and difference but also an understanding of similarities. Everyone needs to learn that someone who may look, get around, or communicate differently—or look the same but learn differently—is more similar to than different from every other human being.

Ms. James and Anita: Dispel Notions of Prejudice

Ms. James is an effective and conscientious fifth-grade teacher. A student in her classroom, Anita, communicates using an iPad and a computer software program that turns her spoken dictation into text. Ms. James has discovered that Anita understands material best when she hears it being read, so Anita typically uses audio books.

Realizing that the other students in the classroom perceive Anita as less intelligent because she uses dictation software, audio books, and an iPad, Ms. James has created an innovative lesson. In a unit during which students choose their own writing topics, she has them dictate their paper using the software Anita uses and then edit their transcripts. Students discover that this different way of writing is not necessarily easier, just different. Ms. James also tells her students that there are many businesspeople, lawyers, and other professionals who dictate letters and other documents as a matter of course. The students now look at Anita's supports in a different light, and have more respect for divergent ways of thinking and doing.

Ms. James *makes difference ordinary* by having all her students learn a different way of doing something. She dispels notions of prejudice around diversity and helps her students understand that a different way of doing something is not an inferior way!

> *The students now look at Anita's supports in a different light, and have more respect for divergent ways of thinking and doing.*

Marianne: Promote Understanding by All

School social worker Marianne epitomizes the way of thinking I'm promoting in this book and is one of my inspirations. A few years ago, when Marianne was in her sixties, her school introduced new inclusive practices. Marianne had seen many educational trends come and go (and sometimes come back again) and could have reacted with jaded indifference. Instead she was collaborative and progressive, open to new ideas even if they would help only one learner. Marianne was an adept active listener and an astute problem solver. She wanted to be an active part of the classrooms in which she worked, strengthening each student's overall education, not just those on her caseload list. Teachers welcomed her into their classrooms, and students welcomed her teaching.

Marianne's curriculum was centered on understanding individual differences and diversity. She also promoted self-esteem by encouraging everyone to be her or his own person. She helped students celebrate their uniqueness. Learning these lessons is just as important as learning history or geography or math.

My grateful thanks to Marianne for inspiring the following unit on understanding and embracing diversity. Special thanks also to Stephanie Harvey and Smokey Daniels for creating and sharing their very relevant and meaningful group discussion format.

> *She dispels notions of prejudice around diversity and helps her students understand that a different way of doing something is not an inferior way!*

Unit on Understanding and Embracing Diversity

When and Why: Present this unit early in the year. Understanding and celebrating individual differences in the classroom enhances group work and student collaboration. It is the foundation on which to build a classroom community.

Initiate: Discuss diversity in terms of culture, family structure, and learning. Identify racial and ethnic percentages in the community in which the school is located and talk about how they have changed over time. Introduce various family structures by having each student identify each member of their family. Tell students that the classroom inquiry and activities in this unit are centered around diversity.

Teach/Model: State that cultural diversity was integral to the founding of the United States of America. Families of various kinds arrived at Ellis Island from many parts of the world speaking many different languages. Lots of people did not understand one another.

In a discussion with a group of adult colleagues (perhaps the teacher in the classroom next door, a special educator, a bilingual teacher, a speech teacher, a social worker, a counselor, a para-educator, a school secretary, a janitor), reveal your and your colleagues' cultural histories and backgrounds, the families in which you grew up, your families now. Allow students to ask questions.

Next, tell students that additional aspects of our diversity are the strengths and challenges we have in learning. These strengths can be thought of as gifts and these challenges can be thought of as disabilities, and everyone in the world has both. Then have the same group of colleagues discuss your various learning strengths (gifts) and challenges (disabilities).

Guided Practice: Have students talk about what they observed you and your colleagues doing during your discussions. Tell them they are now going to have a similar discussion with a small group of their classmates.

Collaborative Practice: Divide students into groups of five. Give each group the following handout itemizing procedures for their discussion

1. Appoint:
   - A facilitator, who will initiate the discussion and ensure that everyone participates.
   - A recorder, who will write down each group member's answers to the questions in step 10. (This group self-assessment will be turned in at the end of the discussion.)
   - A sharer, who will summarize your discussion orally when the whole class reconvenes.
   - A media master, who will help each group member create an individual graphic profile of his or her cultural background, family structure, and learning strengths and challenges.
   - A publisher, who will, in collaboration with the publishers from the other groups, summarize this activity in a blog entry on the class website.
2. With the facilitator's guidance, have each member of your group share his or her cultural background, especially things that are unique.
3. With the facilitator's guidance, have each member of your group share her or his family structure, especially things that are unique.
4. With the facilitator's guidance, have each member of your group discuss his or her strengths and gifts, especially things that are unique.
5. With the facilitator's guidance, have each member of your group discuss her or his challenges and disabilities, especially things that are unique.

Chapter **Ten**

Bring It All Together

Successful Inclusive Schooling Leads to Successful Educational Outcomes

Possibility turns into success when teachers, family members, other educational team members, and the student become agents for the change they wish to see, and together they facilitate the learning processes that best match the student's abilities and needs. They also need to keep up to date on practices that better support diverse learners, consider student priorities, create action plans, and meet the steps and goals specified in those plans.

Joelle: Be the Agent for the Change You Wish to See

Joelle loves computers, the Internet, music, the band One Direction, YouTube, the Food Network, desserts, and languages, and is intrigued by people. She also has Williams syndrome, a genetic developmental challenge. Her mother, Darian, is passionate about inclusive education for all children and wants to help families like hers work collaboratively with educators and schools to promote successful practices. She feels inclusive education makes the world a better place and we would have fewer school and world problems if it were a common practice.

> *She feels inclusive education makes the world a better place and we would have fewer school and world problems if it were a common practice.*

When I met Darian, she told me she loves the way I characterize a disability as simply another attribute, one characteristic among many interests, passions, and challenges that make people who they are. She also confessed that she sometimes feels all alone in her public quest to promote inclusive education, that most families do so privately, invisibly.

In their research into Williams syndrome Darian and her husband, Dean, learned that kids with disabilities should not get lost in a resource room, that the general education classroom was the way to go. However, when Darian began attending inclusive education conferences, no one told her *how* to pursue inclusion or introduced her to the tools and strategies to make it happen. She realized she would need to *be a proactive agent for the change she wished to see.*

She realized she would need to be a proactive agent for the change she wished to see.

One of Darian's major concerns was that Joelle had been pulled out of the general education classroom from kindergarten through third grade for much of her instruction. In fourth grade the pullout was continued and Joelle wasn't making progress in reading and other basic skills. Darian and Dean were very worried.

During the time Joelle was in fourth grade, Darian attended a dynamic presentation about the nuts and bolts of how to help students with disabilities access the general education curriculum given by Robin, an assistive technology specialist, and Erin, a parent and international speaker with years of experience. Together, after a decade of informally helping families and schools, the pair created an educational consulting firm called Bridges to Life Consulting (see www .bridgestolifeconsulting.com), specializing in the use of accommodations and assistive technology to build bridges of learning for students to make progress in the general curriculum. During the session, Darian learned about assistive technology devices, computer software, netbooks (mini–laptop computers), and drop-and-drag assignments necessary to support effective inclusion in the general education curriculum. Robin and Erin also suggested that important areas for Joelle to focus on were socialization and music therapy, so Darian suggested that Joelle's educational team incorporate opportunities for socialization and music therapy into Joelle's day.

Darian called Robin and Erin to create an inclusive plan of support for Joelle. Darian, Dean, Robin, and Erin asked to review the fourth-grade curriculum in advance but their request was denied. When they reviewed Joelle's report cards and other assessment data they were shocked to discover they didn't contain any quantitative data about her progress. All it contained were platitudes that spoke more to her personality than her progress as a student.

Joelle's fourth-grade teacher was new to teaching and not a good match with Joelle's learning style and needs. For example, he sent Joelle home with words on a piece of paper with no explanation of what she was to do with them. Darian again became the agent for the change she wished to see. She created PowerPoint slides that included the words, pictures of what the words represented, and an example of their use in a sentence. She shared these with the teacher, but the teacher did not reciprocate by implementing any adaptations or supports for Joelle. Darian suggested that Joelle be able to use a computer to write but received no response.

The plan that Darian, Dean, Robin, and Erin created for Joelle was not being followed, and the supports she needed in order to be able to learn were not being provided. Her school day was fragmented, and the segregated, isolated interventions the school provided had nothing to do with the curriculum. Darian, Dean, and Robin set up a meeting with the school principal, the special education director, and Joelle's teachers and asked that Joelle's support plan be reworked to include accountability measures. During the meeting, school personnel became very defensive and questioned Robin and Erin's right to be involved.

At least once a week Joelle said she didn't like school. She had social relationships but was treated like a mascot rather than a true friend.

Over the course of the school year, Darian had several meetings with the principal about Joelle's academic plan. The principal decided to bring in the Special Education Director of area schools to observe Joelle's current school day and evaluate the services she was receiving. The director told Darian and Dean they needed to trust the school. Darian was not allowed to observe her daughter's classroom. Joelle's progress continued to deteriorate. She was in fourth grade and reading at a pre-first-grade level when Darian's research showed she should be reading at grade level.

The school started to prepare for fifth grade. Their recommendation consisted primarily of a segregated program that was a repeat of the system they had in place for fourth grade. Darian knew that Joelle needed an inclusive education to advance, but it was not going to happen in this school. Darian felt helpless and defeated—and heart-broken. Her physical and emotional health began to suffer, as did Joelle's. Things needed to change. But they didn't.

Darian and Dean took a bold step. They contacted a nearby private all-girls school with an outstanding academic reputation and learned the school had success-fully included a girl with Down syndrome in its general education curriculum. The headmaster met with Robin, Erin, and Margaret (the general education teacher whose classroom Joelle would attend) at Darian and Dean's home. They agreed they would work as a team to create accommodations for Joelle within the general education curriculum. Serving Joelle's best interests was the goal, all options open.

> *In one year, she not only advanced socially but also made three full years of academic gains!*

Nevertheless, Darian and Dean gave the existing school (which their two other daughters also attended) one more chance. They created a fifteen-page IEP for Joelle, entirely within the general education classroom and curriculum; it specified that they, her parents, would also provide remedial educational supports outside school. The meeting to discuss the IEP was attended only by the school's principal and the vice principal. They told Darian and Dean the school could no longer accommodate Joelle; she was being kicked out!

Therefore, Joelle switched to the all-girls private school they had met with previously. When Joelle began attending the new school, her and Darian's health and happiness immediately improved. Darian, Dean, their neighbors, and people in the community all noticed Joelle's new maturity and confidence. In one year, she not only advanced socially but also made *three full years of academic gains*!

Joelle's educators now include a general education teacher well versed in inclusive practices, a reading consultant, Robin and Erin as consultants, a reading specialist, and a para-educator who adapts the curriculum for Joelle's schoolwork but is not present in the classroom. When other students asked why Joelle was permitted to use a computer, the teacher replied it was because handwriting was difficult for Joelle. No one ever asked about it again.

Joelle is now learning about the Barbarians and Greek mythology, reciting poetry, and spelling—*and she loves reading*! She (not her parents) does her homework every night. Her spirit is glowing. She is learning. She is growing. Sometimes she struggles. But she has a teacher who knows how to teach. As Joelle and Dean were walking the dog one recent morning, Joelle told her dad, "I really like school now; I was bored before."

At Joelle's old school people often told Darian and Dean how cute Joelle was. Joelle's new school is focused on Joelle's academic abilities and socialization and how best to meet her needs in the general education classroom. Darian now warns people to be wary of "benevolence" like that demonstrated at Joelle's old school. The secret is to work on social relationships and make real friends. Everyone needs friends, and friends are not paid.

Recently Joelle was invited to a birthday party at an ice-skating rink. Dean took her, went inside with her, and began putting on his skates. Joelle said, "Dad, why are you here? You need to leave; I'm at a party!" Situation normal!

> *The secret is to work on social relationships and make real friends. Everyone needs friends, and friends are not paid.*

Matthew: Operate from Support, Not Fear

Matthew is an alert, energetic, hands-on learner. I met him as a fourth-grader in a suburban elementary school near a big city. His interests include pizza, school, adult attention, praise, reading, books, mathematics, making up his own math problems, music, playing drums, nature CDs, computers, humor, and movies. He also has intellectual challenges and needs objects around him that support sensory integration.

He communicates during activities through words, pictures with words, pictures, and his actions. He is quite social and wants to communicate with others. Matt likes both his fellow students and the adults he comes in contact with. He is able to advocate for himself, possesses determination, and seeks respect and positive support from others. If he is not receiving positive attention, he sometimes resorts to challenging behavior as communication; for example, he might leave the classroom. Educators who respect him, build a relationship with him, give him positive attention, and believe in him are able to work with him successfully. Matt does best when he is allowed to determine how he wants to exercise a skill or fulfill a responsibility.

I observed Matt several times during fourth grade. That year his teachers had increased the amount of inclusive education he received and the inclusive environments he was part of, and they and I focused on supports that would contribute to and enhance Matt's learning. Providing inclusive education for students like Matt was a new approach for the school, and it was a learning process for educators, administrators, Matt's family, and most certainly Matt!

When Matt was in fifth grade, I was called in as a consultant again because some new adventuresome behaviors started for Matt that were other forms of communication. For example, he tripped other students on the bus and sometimes refused to comply with his teachers' requests or follow directions. When I observed Matt in the classroom, it was obvious that his special education teacher was uncomfortable with him being placed in general education environments due to her lack of background and experience with the practice of inclusive education.

I talked with Matt's educational team about providing positive behavior supports and told them the best way to help him learn was to develop a great relationship with him, integrate his favorite interests into subjects and activities, and offer positive reinforcement for positive behaviors. I also conducted a training session on inclusive education, universal learning design, differentiated instruction, and individual accommodation. Most of the team members seemed to understand my suggestions, but the next time I observed Matt in the classroom, I noticed his special education teacher hadn't changed any of her support practices. She remained uncomfortable with his inclusive education placement.

Change can be very difficult, but we must all remain committed to inclusive education! Matt is now a sixth-grader in middle school—a chance for a fresh start. His new teacher, Ms. Monroe, is experienced and assured. She has high expectations for Matt and is very natural around him. In addition, Matt receives support from a male para-educator with whom he has a great relationship. He now has better peer models, positive social relationships with other boys, and better communication skills. His academic skills are also improving, which has led to improved self-esteem. These are all winning combinations.

Matt's educational team celebrates small steps (which his family modeled) and is exploring creative new ways to increase his participation in school and community activities. For example, he recently had a role in a Civil War reenactment, and he has sung a solo in a school concert. Matt's parents, Lance and Susan, have always had high expectations for him in the community. For one thing, he is an active member of his church. His parents feel that inclusive education has helped Matt take a big step forward and make more apparent gains. He now rides the general school bus and goes to his classroom on his own. He attended an inclusive camp last summer and one of his counselors said he'd be back next summer if Matt would be!

> *Keeping an eye toward the future has a huge impact on a diverse learner's dream to be a fully participating, respected citizen.*

I am thrilled for both Matt and Joelle and the new strides they are taking in their journeys. Their stories are the inspiration for the Student Priorities/Action Plan at a Glance form below. Keeping an eye toward the future has a huge impact on a diverse learner's dream to be a fully participating, respected citizen. It is my wish to make *everyone's* dreams a reality. Please join me in making this wish come true! With the active participation of all teachers and all parents (who are their sons' and daughters' teachers first and always), we will create an inclusive world.

Student Priorities/Action Plan at a Glance

Student Name: _____

Student Profile: _____

1. Where does _____ want to live one day? How can school experiences prepare him/her to be able to do so?

2. How does _____ want to earn a living? How can school experiences help her/him be able to do so?

3. How does _____ like to have fun? What are his/her favorite forms of recreation? How can school experiences support his/her ability to engage in these activities for a lifetime?

What action steps are necessary to realize these priorities? Who will take these steps, by when?

Action Step	Who Will Take It?	By When?

Example

Student Priorities/Action Plan at a Glance

Student Name: _Micah_

Student Profile: Micah is an eleventh-grader who is preparing to go on to college. He enjoys working with computers, playing basketball, and playing video games. He also has Asperger syndrome.

1. Where does Micah want to live one day? How can school experiences prepare him to be able to do so?

    Micah would like to be married and live in a house or apartment. The courses he wants to take next year are Family and Consumer Sciences, Consumer Math, and Health. As a stepping-stone to living in the community, he has an opportunity to sublet an apartment on the local college campus this summer. He will have a roommate who is already living in the apartment.

2. How does Micah want to earn a living? How can school experiences help him be able to do so?

    He wants to work with computers. Next year he will have a part-time work-study position entering data for a local business. He will also take a business technology course. After he graduates, he wants to get a business technology degree from a university.

3. How does Micah like to have fun? What are his favorite forms of recreation? How can school experiences support his ability to engage in these activities for a lifetime?

    Micah likes basketball and computer games. His family took out a YMCA membership for Micah last year. He plays basketball in the YMCA gym and swims in the YMCA pool. His parents are going to look for video arcades close to his job, his home, and the YMCA where he can play computer games with a friend.

What action steps are necessary to realize these priorities? Who will take these steps, by when?

Action Step	Who Will Take It?	By When?
Register for Family & Consumer Sciences, Consumer Math, Business Technology, & Health courses	Micah, with his school counselor	May 15th
Sublet apartment on college campus for summer	Micah and family	ASAP
Set up a computer work-study job at a local business	Work-study teacher	In progress, results need to be in place by September
Teach Micah to use public transportation	Micah and family	In progress, results need to be shared with team in September
Identify video arcades near home, YMCA, and job	Micah and family	In progress, results to be shared with team in September
Explore colleges that have business technology programs and student support services that are a good match for Micah	Micah and team	Early next school year

Final **Thoughts**

As we near the end of our exploration of ways to achieve positive student outcomes in inclusive classrooms, we need to reflect on the schools of today and the schools of the future. How can we make a difference in the days of Common Core State Standards, RtI, teaching toward the test, comparing test scores with other school districts, and returning to ability-based groupings? We can make a difference and make learning work for *all* students by understanding and embracing the diversity of our learners, designing creative instruction, and always keeping an eye on our students' present and future needs.

The introduction to this book posed several important questions, to which the subsequent chapters suggested answers. Let's look again at those questions and summarize how teachers can turn possibility into success.

How do we make all the changes taking place in education work for rather than against what we know is good for learners?

Schools today need to adopt philosophies and practices that embrace learning ownership for all students. *Every student can and will learn.* Philosophy guides action; if we adopt this philosophy as our watchword, learning will happen.

Clearly, making the Common Core State Standards our friend by stepping up our preparation, innovation, practice, and assessment in order to make learning work for all students results in better teaching. The scary part is that improving what we do means ridding ourselves of comfortable but ineffective practices and embracing challenging but effective practices.

We must view the IEP as another friend. In a world of larger classrooms and a resulting tendency to fall back on ability grouping, the IEP protects individual integrity. Universally designed learning, differentiated instruction, and individual accommodation help every student in the classroom. The student we think we can do the least with will do the most to make us proud.

Success in the classroom requires owning every student in it, ditching the outdated notion that somebody else will take care of *those* students. Let's be done with the days of *your students and my students* and celebrate the philosophy and practice of educating

> **W**e can make a difference and make learning work for all students by understanding and embracing the diversity of our learners, designing creative instruction, and always keeping an eye on our students' present and future needs.

our students. It will radically change how we view, teach, support, and assess everyone in the classroom.

How do we keep the art of teaching intact while meeting its requirements as a science?

It's tragic when as educators we find ourselves teaching toward a test to ensure we meet the standards. We enter the education profession in order to practice the art of teaching and can be overwhelmed by ever-increasing demands to treat it as a science. Teachers caught up solely in the science of teaching become less passionate, perhaps even bored; they lose the will to make learning come to life and work for everyone. Students with bored teachers become bored with learning. The secret is to plan creatively to keep the art of teaching intact at the same time as addressing the scientific requirements!

> *The secret is to plan creatively to keep the art of teaching intact at the same time as addressing the scientific requirements!*

Role-plays, learning centers, literature circles, inquiry circles, cooperative learning, thematic units, multiple-intelligence learning, hands-on learning, project-based instruction, experiential instruction, student-created lessons, teacher-student lesson planning, games, teambuilding, equitable peer tutors/cross-age peer tutors, active listening, group problem solving, peer advocacy, adult-student teams, and lunch bunches (approaches to student collaboration and leadership discussed in Chapter 6) are a great way to start.

After planning creatively, we need to verify which Common Core State Standards are being met and what needs to be tweaked. (The good-news surprise is how little tweaking will be necessary.) This "back-mapping" approach to planning takes a bit more time in the beginning, but it quickly becomes common—and efficient—practice. It is also much more effective, and both teachers and students have more fun!

How do we get teachers and leaders to embrace rather than begrudge meeting the needs of all learners?

Today's teachers have many added responsibilities, and not all of them seem student-centered. It is easy to passively resist *anything* new, even things that are beneficial. Many of the best and most promising practices championed in this book are not part of the initial professional training many teachers receive. We must persuade them—through books, websites, professional development programs, and classroom visits—to be open to innovations, even if they benefit only one learner, and to stay the course. *We are in it for the students.*

How do we learn from the ways students experience and use technology in their daily lives?

Even though technology is evolving at speeds faster than we can keep up with and many of us approach technology as immigrants, our students are natives. Those of us with teenagers at home know the best way to reach them is to text, not call. Why shouldn't students improve their writing skills by texting or through online written conversations? Why shouldn't learning have some of the same components found in video and computer games? The lesson plan format in Chapter 1 embraces technology as a universal design strategy for providing access to learning through representation, engagement, and expression. Technology is a useful support tool and an excellent way to recapture disinterested and disengaged learners. And it often opens doors wider for learners with disabilities. Use it effectively for all!

How do we focus on best and most promising practices and successful learning for all students during their entire school career, learning that will enhance their quality of life?

Recently I made a presentation in Memphis, Tennessee. I'd never spent any time there before, so I extended my stay and did a little sightseeing: Graceland, Sun Studio, Beale Street, the Stax Museum of American Soul Music, the Gibson Guitar Factory, and the Rock and Soul Museum. An avid music lover, I was in my glory!

However, the most moving place I visited was the National Civil Rights Museum, on the grounds of the Lorraine Motel, where Martin Luther King was assassinated. After viewing a number of poignant and informative displays, I found myself alone in one of the rooms (although the museum was full of visitors). In the room was an old-fashioned bus, its door open. I walked on. A statue of Rosa Parks, sitting near the front, took me by surprise. I froze for a moment, then sat on a seat near her and cried. Rosa Parks' brave act was a landmark in the fight to eliminate racial segregation, and the message she sent is in support of all disenfranchised people.

> *When students experience segregation every day in the primary place they learn, their school, they graduate believing that's the way the world should be as well.*

I am shocked that the segregation of people with disabilities remains commonplace in our schools and communities. I have testified in countless court cases undertaken on behalf of students fighting to be included in general education classrooms in an educational system that continues to believe they need to be with people like them to learn. We need more people like Rosa Parks. We need to emulate her bravery and leadership and take on—and abolish—one of the major instances of segregation that still exist. When students experience segregation every day in the primary place they learn, their school, they graduate believing that's the way the world should be as well. If segregation is acceptable in their school, students come to believe that people with disabilities belong in different rooms, at different lunch tables, only with one another. Segregation begets segregation.

The tools to make inclusive education work are in this book. I would be honored if you incorporate them into your classroom practice. You have accomplished the first step by reading. The next step is believing and doing. The people whose stories I tell in this book are making it happen; you can too!

Works Cited

Brown, Lou, Elise Frattura Kampschroer, Alice Udvari-Solner, Patrick Schwarz, Pat VanDeventer, Grace Courchane, Kate Stanton, Lisa Terlau, and Jack Jorgensen. 1990. *Educational Programs for Students with Severe Intellectual Disabilities*. Vol. 20. Madison, WI: Madison Metropolitan School District.

CAST. 2012. "CAST Universal Design for Learning." Wakefield, MA: CAST. www.cast.org.

Cooper, J. David, Janet McWilliams, Irene Boschken, and Lynne Pistochini. 2001. *Classroom Teaching Skills*. Lexington, KY: D.C. Heath.

Fein, Deborah. 2011. *The Neuropsychology of Autism*. Bethesda, MD: Oxford University Press.

Fisher, Douglas, Nancy Frey, and Carol Rothenberg. 2010. *Implementing RTI with English Learners*. Bloomington, IN: Solution Tree.

Fulk, Barbara, and Kathy King. 2001. "Classwide Peer Tutoring at Work." *Teaching Exceptional Children* 34(2): 49–53.

Gardner, Howard. 2011. *Frames of Mind: The Theory of Multiple Intelligences*. 3rd ed. New York: Basic Books.

Golenbock, Peter, and Paul Bacon. 1992. *Teammates*. San Anselmo, CA: Sandpiper.

Grandin, Temple. 2011. *The Way I See It: A Personal Look at Autism and Asperger's*. 2nd ed. Arlington, TX: Future Horizons.

Harvey, Stephanie, and Harvey Daniels. 2009. *Comprehension and Collaboration: Inquiry Circles in Action*. Portsmouth, NH: Heinemann.

Individuals with Disabilities Education Act (IDEA). Section 601. Public Law. 2004.

Kluth, Paula, and Patrick Schwarz. 2008. *"Just Give Him the Whale!" 20 Ways to Use Fascinations, Areas of Expertise, and Strengths to Support Students with Autism.* Baltimore, MD: Brookes.

_____. 2010. *Pedro's Whale.* Baltimore, MD: Brookes.

Kohn, Alfie. 2006. *Beyond Discipline: From Compliance to Community.* Alexandria, VA: Association for Supervision and Curriculum Development.

Mager, Robert F. 1988. *Making Instruction Work.* California: David S. Lake.

McCall, Jeremiah. 2011. *Gaming the Past: Using Video Games to Teach Secondary History.* New York: Routledge.

O'Brien, John, Jack Pearpoint, and Lynda Kahn. 2010. *The PATH and Maps Handbook: Person-Centered Ways to Build Community.* Montreal: Inclusion.

Ricketts, Cliff, and John Ricketts. 2010. *Leadership: Personal Development and Career Success.* Clifton, NY: Delmar Cengage Learning.

Schumm, J. S., S. Vaughn, and J. Harris. 1998. "Pyramid Power for Collaborative Planning for Content Area Instruction." *Teaching Exceptional Children* 29(6): 62–66.

Schwarz, Patrick. 2006. *From Disability to Possibility: The Power of Inclusive Classrooms.* Portsmouth, NH: Heinemann.

Theoharis, George, and Julie Causton-Theoharis. 2010. "Include, Belong, Learn." *Educational Leadership* 68(2): 35–38.

Tomlinson, Carol Ann. 2004. *How to Differentiate Instruction in Mixed-Ability Classrooms.* 2nd ed. Alexandria, VA: Association for Supervision and Curriculum Development.

Wiggins, G., and J. McTighe. 1998. *Understanding by Design.* Alexandria: Association for Supervision and Curriculum Development.

Zemelman, Steve, Harvey Daniels, and Arthur Hyde. 2012. *Best Practice: Bringing Standards to Life in America's Classrooms.* 4th ed. Portsmouth, NH: Heinemann.